FEVER

Book 4 of the FADE Series™

By

Kailin Gow

Fever (FADE #4)

Published by Sparklesoup Inc.

First Published 2012

For information, please contact:

Sparklesoup.com

Kailin Gow

Henceforth space by itself, and time by itself, are doomed to fade away into mere shadows, and only a kind of union of the two will preserve an independent reality. – Hermann Minkowski

PROLOGUE

I'm in the treatment center. I know that instantly as I look around. Though calling it that is a joke. There's nothing we can do to treat people. All we can do is bring them in, quarantine them, and do our best to care for them. Even that, we can't do so much of now. We don't have the people.

I stand there watching as the staff work, shepherding people into tiny rooms, stripping them off and rinsing them down with the best disinfectant sprays we have. A child wails at the sting of the disinfectant mix. An old woman complains about the indignity of having to do it like this, in front of strangers. About the damage being dunked in more disinfectant is doing to her pictures of her family.

She's right. There's no dignity here. Not for anyone. The Fever doesn't leave any room for it. It doesn't leave any room for so many things. It takes people and it makes

4

them mad, makes them do things that they would never do. Then it burns them up, a little at a time, until there isn't anything left of them.

And all we can do is spray people with disinfectant.

I'm the president of this country. The most powerful woman in the free world, if anything is truly free anymore, now that the Fever has destroyed so much. My abilities let me do things that even most of the others around me don't have the power to do. I'm the strongest of us, the most politically powerful, probably one of the smartest.

None of that matters when it comes to the Fever. I'm as helpless as everyone else. I can't do anything to cure it. All I can do is find enough "doctors" to try to keep the few remaining healthy people from contracting it. It isn't enough. I should be able to do something. People are *relying* on me.

Jack's there by my side then. The way he always is. The way I need him to be.

"Celes, Grayson and John say the machine is nearly ready."

"That's good," I say, even though I can feel the tension building in me. The machine is our best hope. Our *only* hope.

"Walk with me?" Jack says, and looking into the deep blue of his eyes, I know what he intends. I nod. We walk out of the medical area, through to the room where the machine waits. It's such an elaborate thing. The best that our technology can produce. Maybe it will give us a chance.

Right now though, I have other things to think about as Jack kisses me. For once, it doesn't matter that Jack is my chief of security. I don't care whether people see us. We've been together since high school, and Jack is about to do something almost impossibly dangerous for all of us. If he succeeds, it will be like the Fever never happened. If he fails...

I hope against hope that he doesn't fail, even while I kiss him for what might be the last time. I cling to him while his lips move over mine, our mouths moving in perfect harmony while his hands drift over my body. I wish we had more time, not to mention a more private room...

"Celes. Jack."

6

We break apart. Grayson is there. He's been helping to work on this project since the start, but it's Jack who has the scores to fulfill the mission. I'm the only one who has scored higher when it comes to resisting the effects of the machine on memory, and Grayson has ganged up with Jack on this one. I'm too precious to go. Which means that the man I love has to go to what could be his death instead.

I can't send him.

"Are we ready?" John follows Grayson into the room. He looks almost eager, but then, he's been trying the hardest of all of us to cure the Fever. He's the one who has seen the most of what it can do. He and Grayson are the ones who have made the machine work, and given us this chance.

Grayson nods. "The coordinates are set for the reconstruction. Whenever you're ready, Jack."

I want to tell him no. I want to tell him that he can't go. That I forbid it as both the woman who loves him and as his president. Yet I know that if I'm truly his president, I have to let him go. And if I love anything else in this world, I have to wish him luck.

Fever (FADE #4)

"Good luck, Jack," I whisper against his lips.

"It's time," Grayson says, looking over at us. He looks almost as torn as I am, but then, Jack is his best friend. And I know how he feels about me too.

Jack nods. "Don't look so worried. If this goes well, you'll hardly notice I'm gone."

It's just like him to make jokes. If this goes well, the world will change, and it will have always been the way it is. A new world. One with Jack in it again, hopefully, but without the Fever. If we've judged this right.

"The coordinates are right?" I ask.

"We've checked a dozen times, Celes," Grayson says. "You've checked them."

I have. I'm just trying to delay the moment when Jack is gone.

"Grayson," Jack calls out as he moves over to the machine. "You remember the promise you made me?"

Grayson nods. "I remember. I'll do it."

"I hope so." He steps into the machine, letting John strap him in. The doctor is careful about it, but even so it just feels wrong. Wrong for Jack to look so calm when in a few moments, the machine is going to disintegrate him utterly.

It's the only way to get where he's going. As a stream of information pulsed along a channel carefully calculated to open in the right spot. Something to be reconstructed. Something to perform our vital mission.

I force myself to stand and watch while John throws the switch...

ONE

I wake with my head on a familiar chest. It's a hard, firm, muscular chest, and I've woken with my head on it before now, but it's still a good feeling to know that Jack's there. I sit up and see the rest of Jack. His usually neat dark hair is tousled on the arm of the couch we're lying on top of, while his athletic body is still encased in his dark working suit. That's a pity.

We're in Wilson Hammond's tower, in the secure suite where his guards deposited us after we failed to kill him. Jack and I have been here before, so that its elegantly minimalist furniture and heat resistant white walls are almost familiar by now. That doesn't make them welcoming though. A beautiful cell is still a cell, even when it's one we've escaped from before.

Jack has his arms around me as I sit there, like he's trying to shelter me from harm. What harm? It actually takes me a moment or two to remember, like everything

10

before today has been a dream, yet when I do, I start to shake Jack, willing him to wake up.

The apocalypse. We're in here because Wilson Hammond, the United States' new president, wanted us out of the way while he began the apocalypse. After everything we went through to try and stop it, it still happened, with fire raining from the sky and people worshipping him like a god. We've been locked in here for days now, while outside… I don't want to think about what has been happening outside.

Yet now, something feels different.

"Jack, come on, wake up."

I finally shake him awake, those icy blue eyes of his flickering open. He smiles up at me for a moment, then, like me, he seems to remember what's happening. He sits up sharply.

"Something has changed."

I can feel it too, but it's good to know that Jack agrees. He's the one who gets flashes of the immediate future. He's the one whose powers run to sensitivity, so that he can pick up on some of what's going on around him. That has been hard, the last few days. We've been here, trapped not so much by the locks as by what's going on outside, grabbing snatched sleep and watching the TV until the signal cut out. And all the time, we've known that outside this building, people have been dying.

"Is it over?" I ask.

Jack looks at me, shakes his head, and then shrugs. "I don't know."

I check my phone. I was surprised when Hammond's men didn't take it from me, but now I can see why. There's no signal, the way there has been no signal for days. If I want to call Grayson, or try to get in touch with Jack's father Sebastian, then I won't be doing it with this.

"So what do we do?" I ask. "We can't just sit here waiting with no news."

I don't say the obvious thing. That unless they made it to the shelters they were heading for, the people we care about could be dead. I don't want to think about that. I have to hope that they made it to their shelters in time, and that those shelters were strong enough.

"It could still be dangerous out there," Jack points out, the way he's pointed it out every time I've asked about leaving. I know he cares about everyone else as much as I do, but more than all of them he cares about me. He wants to keep me safe. Even if it means forcing me to ride out the apocalypse in Wilson Hammond's shelter. How long does the apocalypse last? A day? A year? How long can we survive here on the contents of our suite's small kitchen?

"Something feels different, Jack. We have to check."

He nods. "I know. We'll go get cleaned up, and then we'll start."

That's easier than I expect it to be. "You're okay with checking?"

"We need to know what's going on," Jack says. He kisses me lightly. "Now hurry up. I want to take a shower. I have a feeling it's the last one I'll get for a while."

I head into the bathroom first, taking with me clothes from drawers embedded in the walls. I don't like taking anything provided by Hammond or his people, but after days wearing the same clothes they're better than the ones I have on. There are tough, hard dark jeans, grey and black sneakers, a t-shirt of pale blue and an off white shirt to go over the top. I take a shower before putting them on, trying to untangle strands of dark hair afterwards with a comb before giving in and tying my hair back.

When I check in the bathroom mirror, my eyes blaze with that hint of golden fire that's a reminder of the power lurking below the surface in me. Despite everything I've been through in the last few days, I have to admit I still look pretty good, like I'm about to go out on a modeling assignment rather than looking at the aftermath of the end of the world. I think back to those days hiding out with Jack in the apartment the Underground assigned us, pretending to be a model while the Others hunted for me. Compared to this, even that seems so simple now.

I come out of the bathroom, while Jack gives me a hungry look as he goes in. I get the feeling, under other circumstances, that he'd be more than happy to keep me in this room with him. Now though, there are more serious things to think about, like getting out. Actually though, that isn't too hard to do. Although Wilson Hammond's advanced materials were enough to stop me once, now, my power has grown to the point where I simply melt my way through the locks on the door. After that, we take the

14

stairs, heading down to the lobby the way we went the last time we escaped from here. Should I be worried that I'm escaping from places often enough that I do it more than once from the same place?

The first thing I notice is how empty the building is. This is meant to be a shelter capable of holding dozens of people, maybe hundreds, but I don't see anyone on the way down to the lobby. Jack doesn't seem to sense anyone, either. The whole place is as quiet as a ghost town, when it should have been busy keeping people safe. Has something gone wrong? It's hard to think that Hammond would have used his whole main shelter just to protect us.

When we get to the lobby, the toughened glass frontage is covered in dust. Completely covered, so that we can't see out. The idea of stepping out there when we can't see what's going on is a daunting one, but Jack and I look at one another and know that we have to. We throw open the doors.

Outside, it's as still as the shelter we've just left. There's a layer of ash over everything, thick and grey, drifting like snow in places. We're in the middle of an industrial park, but there's no industry. There's no noise. There's nothing but a silence so absolute that it makes me want to scream just to break it. We walk out to the main road, trying to catch sight of someone as we get close to the rest of the city, but there's no one that we can see. No one. Not in the houses. Not in the stores. It's like the entire population of the city is gone.

"We have to find Grayson," I say.

"And the Faders, my father, my uncle." Jack pauses, looking around. "Someone. Other people must have survived. There were shelters. People must have been in them, or there was no point in building them."

I nod. I know that, even though it's hard to believe, looking around to see nothing but empty streets.

"You're right," I say. "I know you're right. I know in our future, the apocalypse happened and an entire population survived to rebuild. It's just..."

"It's too quiet?" Jack guesses.

I nod. "I guess we'll just have to keep looking, though we won't get very far if we try it on foot."

The first vehicle we come across is a jeep, abandoned by the side of the road. Amazingly, the keys are still in the ignition. Whoever left this left it in a hurry. Jack tries to start it, but the engine just sputters and dies. He tries again. After a minute or two, it becomes clear that it isn't going to work. Maybe that's why the owner didn't mind leaving their keys behind.

We keep moving, and soon we find a mall, or what's left of it. Most of the roof seems to be gone from it, while the outer walls are badly damaged. I look at Jack.

"We're going to need supplies," I say. "It could be a while before we find anyone."

He agrees, and we head inside. It occurs to me that technically we're about to loot a store, but I'm not worried about getting into trouble now. Trouble means people. In any case, it's better than starving. We find a store that has a couple of small backpacks in it, along with some camping supplies. We take those, then head over into a grocery store. Most of what was there is gone, but there's still one refrigerator with food in it. We both fill up our bags from it.

I'd feel better if we were both armed too, but there aren't any weapons to be found. We'll just have to rely on our abilities if we run into trouble. What worries me is that there are no people here. A mall would be a natural place for people to survive after a disaster, but there's still no sign of anyone.

We leave the mall, moving down the street to a car dealership. Most of the vehicles there are in bad shape, flipped over, badly damaged, or simply covered in that fine ash that seems to get everywhere. If it's in their engines, they're worthless. Jack picks one of the cars, and quickly breaking into the office gives us the key. Again though, when he tries to start it, nothing happens.

He pops the hood, and an idea comes to me. I put my hand on the engine, calling up the barest spark of power. It leaps through the engine, and in an instant, the car is running. I have to admit, I'm almost as shocked as Jack when it works.

"It looks like your power can do plenty more than destroy things," Jack says. "It looks like, if you can direct the power you call up, it can do a lot."

"Maybe," I say, not quite convinced.

"It's a gift," Jack says. "You just have to know how to use it. And we do have a working car now thanks to you."

"True," I say, and I am a little proud of that. It's nice to know that I can do something with my abilities other than kill people. "So, where are we heading?"

That's the question, of course. Where can we go? Where will there be people? Anywhere? We have to hope so. We have to hope that being here hasn't changed things already. That there is still a world for us to save.

TWO

Jack doesn't hesitate when I ask him where we're going. Instead, he sets out the situation calmly, clearly.

"Grayson went after Johnny," he says, "but we don't know if he succeeded, or even if he was able to get to Location Ten before things got too difficult. If he *did* succeed, then he might have tried to ride out the apocalypse in Location Ten, but he might also have tried to make it to a more secure fallback position. If he couldn't make it there, or if something went wrong, then he would have tried to do the same thing. Even if he rode out the initial apocalypse, he might be doing what we're doing and moving on."

"So you're saying that there's no way of knowing where Grayson is?" I ask.

To my surprise, Jack shakes his head. "What I'm saying is that the odds say that Location Ten is a bad idea.

There are other places that Grayson is more likely to be, along with Sebastian and my uncle."

I get the feeling that Jack knows exactly where those places will be, too. "So where will they have gone?"

Jack starts to creep the car along the street. We aren't moving quickly, perhaps because the layer of ash is as hard to drive on as snow or sand.

"Grayson's a Fader, and he's probably with more Faders. In a situation like this, there's only one place *to* go. Location Thirteen."

"Location Thirteen?" I repeat, shaking my head.

"What is it?" Jack asks.

"I was just wondering how many of these Locations you have. And if you couldn't come up with some better names for them."

That gets a smile from Jack. "Numbers are more secure. It means people can't guess anything about them from the name. As for how many... even I'm not sure. A lot. You saw the maps."

I nod. We looked at a map of possible shelters for people. A lot of the Locations would have been on it. "So,"

I ask. "What's so special about Location Thirteen? I take it you don't have a Location set up just for the apocalypse."

Though in truth, most of the really solid ones were set up with just that in mind.

"Location Thirteen is where you go when things turn odd," Jack says. "When there's a real crisis, or a major disaster… well, it's time for Location Thirteen."

"That wasn't where people went when the Others destroyed Location Six," I point out.

Jack brings the car around a corner, heading in the direction of the freeway. "That was bad, but it wasn't the kind of thing I mean. And there were still plenty of other Locations to fall back on . Thirteen is where you go when things get very… weird."

Jack can see flashes of the future. He can move faster than most people. He can touch me when there's power pouring out of me without being burned. He can be healed by my power. What exactly qualifies as 'weird' for him? Aside from this whole situation, obviously?

"So it's the place where you all go when the situation gets so strange that you need help the other Locations can't give you?" I guess.

Jack nods. "Exactly. It's not normally even a functioning Location. It's just like a… backup, I guess. If you need other Faders, then normally you go to a different Location, but when things get too strange for that, it has to be Location Thirteen." Jack sighs. "I guess there are going to be a lot of Faders there right now. I hope so, anyway."

"So we go to Location Thirteen too?" I ask. It seems like the only thing we can do now. We were meant to stop the apocalypse. We failed. *I* failed, because I wouldn't let Jack shoot Wilson Hammond in cold blood. Now all we can do is try to deal with everything that happens afterwards. Try to stop it leading inevitably to the Fever.

"We go to Location Thirteen," Jack agrees. He's still moving the car along cautiously. It's a nice one, a family car with plenty of space in it, but I guess Jack is mostly used to sports cars and military vehicles. He probably doesn't trust it yet. "Getting there could be the hard part, though."

"Why?" I ask. "Where is it?"

"It's not too far from Location Six, where we first tried to Fade you."

23

Fever (FADE #4)

"The Nevada Desert?" I have a lot of memories of that desert. Not all of them are good. There's the attempt to Fade me, the realization that my life to date had been a lie, the attack by the Others that resulted in the destruction of the base... it's going to be hard going back. And not just for personal reasons, either.

"Jack," I point out, "it's a *long* way to the Nevada Desert. If the entire country is like... like *this*, then how do we get there?"

"It's clear across the country," Jack agrees, "but that can't stop us, Celes. This car will do for now, but we'll have to keep a lookout for something better to help us make the journey. A plane or a long range helicopter would be ideal, but for now, this car can at least get us moving in the right direction. It's better than walking, and a lot better than staying still doing nothing."

Jack has a point there. We could just sit in Wilson Hammond's tower, waiting for either the food to run out or the Beast within him to want us dead, but if we actually want to survive, if we want to do something useful, then the car is what we have for now.

Jack keeps driving, the road still slippery with ash as we go along past houses and stores, a community center and a library. We still haven't seen anyone in the street. Maybe there isn't anyone left to see. What will we do if we're the only ones left? No, I have to keep thinking that there will be more than that. Even if we came back to change things, I have to keep believing that there are other people out there.

That's when I see something that might just be a sign of them. A flash of light, reflecting off the car's rear view mirror. For a second, I think it must just be the sun, or something reflecting off one of the windows of the buildings around us, yet this seems different somehow. Particularly when it comes again. It's a flash of light, and it seems to be coming from one of the nearby buildings.

"Jack?" I say. "Did you see that? That light?"

Jack nods, and I can see from his expression that he's already in that calculating space he goes to when danger might be near.

"Yes. Normally, I'd say that we should keep going, because getting to Location Thirteen has to be our priority, but…"

Fever (FADE #4)

"But there might be people in there," I finish for him. Despite everything, we can't just abandon people in the middle of a ruined city like this. They might be hurt. They might need our help. They might also be able to help us.

Jack swings the car around carefully, bringing it up to the curb by the building the light seems to have come from. It's the old library, the doors of which are hanging open.

"If there are people in there," he says, "then they might have information about what has happened, but we need to be careful, Celes."

"I'll be careful," I promise him, hopping out of the car. "But Jack, it's probably nothing. That, or its just ordinary people. We probably don't have a lot to be afraid of."

Jack moves up beside me quickly. He puts a hand on my shoulder. "We don't *know* what there is to be afraid of. That's the point. We have a whole town that's practically empty. We don't know what happened to the people here during the apocalypse, and we *really* don't know what might be in there. After something like this, even normal things are dangerous, Celes. People, animals... they'll be scared, hungry, probably desperate. So we're going to be careful."

I nod again. I think Jack's overreacting, because with my powers, I have the tools to stay safe against most things, while Jack is an expert when it comes to violent situations. Maybe that's why I agree with him though. He's the expert. He's spent so long now keeping me safe that I'm not going to take risks when he says to be careful.

We move a little closer to the open door.

"If there are people there, what do we do?" I ask. "If they need help, then we have to at least try to help them."

Jack nods. "If there are people, then helping them is a priority."

I'd almost expected him not to say that. I'd thought that for Jack, the mission might come first so much that we'd have to abandon anyone we found. But that's the thing with Jack. He can be completely hard and focused one moment, totally gentle the next. It's part of why I care about him so much.

27

Fever (FADE #4)

"If we're very lucky," Jack says, "they'll be able to help us as much as we help them. We have some supplies, but we'll need more than this if we can't find a better way to Location Thirteen than driving."

That makes a kind of sense. We move up to the doors together. Jack's very careful not to stand directly in front of them. Instead, he steps to the side of the frame, like he's expecting something to come out shooting at any moment. He even pulls me there with him when I don't do the same. This close to him, I can smell the strong, masculine scent of him and feel the thrill of carefully controlled danger that comes just from being around him. Even the power within me flickers, the way it so often does when I'm near Jack. Everything about him calls to me when he's like this.

"What is it?" I ask him. "What do you see?"

Jack's precognition doesn't reach far into the future. As far as I know, there isn't anyone whose abilities do let them see very far. We thought that Johnny could, but it turned out he was just remembering his time working with us in the future. Maybe the weight of human choices gets too much beyond a few seconds, the way you can't predict the weather too far in advance because there are too many things going on.

What I do know is that when it comes to things a few seconds ahead, Jack is pretty accurate. Especially when those few seconds are going to contain danger. It's one of the things that makes him so good in a fight, because there isn't anything unexpected for him.

"What is it, Jack?" I repeat.

"I'm not sure," he says. "I just get the feeling that whatever we're going to find in there, it isn't going to be pleasant."

"Does that mean we shouldn't go in?" I ask. "If there's a threat…"

Jack shakes his head. "Even if it's dangerous, it's still the first sign of living things we've had since we left the tower. It might be able to tell us more about what's going on, no matter what it is. We need to go in."

FOUR

Jack's hand goes to the waistband of his pants and he pulls out a gun, a high caliber semi-automatic pistol that isn't quite the same as the weapon Hammond's men took from him.

"I took it from the store in the mall," Jack explains in answer to my questioning look, before slipping into the library. I don't know if leading with a gun would be the right strategy normally, because if it turns out that there are ordinary people in here, then they're more likely to panic when they see the weapon, but I trust Jack. I trust his senses. If he says that there is danger ahead, then there's probably danger ahead.

We head deeper into the library, past blank shelves of books, lit through a skylight in addition to the windows. That only seems to add to the shadows the book shelves cast, turning the place into a maze lit by dappled patches of light. We pad silently towards the far corner of the

Kailin Gow

building, where it seems like the flashes we spotted came from. There's another door there, with *Reading Room* over it in elegant lettering.

There's another flash of light, glowing beneath the door. At least, I *think* there is. It's hard to tell, with the light and shadows of the library confusing things. It's something, anyway, which is why we move over to that inner door. It's already ajar, and this close to it I can smell an odd scent. Like copper and burning plastic, mixed in with burning paper and other things. Other things I know the scent of only too well, because it's a scent that still comes to me whenever I think of all the people I've killed with my power.

It's the scent of burning flesh. A scent that comes complete with a scream, which cuts through the silence of the library before fading to a bubbling gurgle and disappearing completely.

We're through the door in an instant. Someone is in trouble, and that means that we can't just stand by. Jack won't, and I won't. Not if there's a chance to help someone. Except that as soon as we get inside, it's easy to see that it's too late to help anyone here. On the floor,

31

there's a pile of charred remains, fire blackened fragments of bone sticking out of a pile of ashes, the remains of a plastic and metal chair melted in with that pile. Whoever this was, and I know from the speed of my own powers that it *could* be the person who screamed, we're too late to help them. Far too late. I don't even know if we'll be able to help ourselves, because what's standing over that pile of burned flesh…

It's larger than a human by a couple of feet, and there's something vaguely reptilian about the way it moves as it sniffs the air. Yet there's also something terrifyingly human about it too. The heart of it seems to be a human torso, and something that might once have been a human head, before horns rose up from it and it changed to accommodate a bestial maw. Ragged, leathery wings stick out from its back, while a long, reptilian tail reaches to the floor. It has scales that shimmer black and purple, like an oil slick, and when it turns to us, its eyes burn with a deep, fiery glow of power.

"Run," Jack says softly, as though hoping that keeping calm will be enough to keep it from attacking. It isn't. The creature's eyes fix on us, and it seems almost to smile before it crouches to lunge at us. "Run, Celes!"

I leap back as the creature pounces, barely making it through the door to the reading room. Jack is already there, and I know that without the kind of speed we both possess, we'd be dead right now. Not that it isn't still an option. Jack fires two shots through the gap of the door, the noise of them deafening after the silence of the library. They don't do anything except buy us a second in which to close the reading room doors.

Which start to glow with power...

"Keep running, Celes!" Jack insists. "It's coming through."

We sprint along the rows of books, but when there's a crash behind me, I can't help looking back for a second. The creature is there, standing in the ruins of the doors it has just destroyed, staring at us. At me. When it runs, it runs with the speed of something that isn't built like a human, and its roar of anger has nothing to do with a human throat.

I push over the nearest bookcases, hoping to slow it down, then sprint for the door using every ounce of extra speed I have. Jack and I skid out of the door, pausing to close it even though the last one didn't slow the creature for long. Even a few seconds is something. Right now, we need all the time we can get.

"The car," Jack says. "Run for the car, Celes."

I don't need him to tell me that again. I sprint for the car, leaping in at the passenger side while Jack takes the driver's seat. He works the key we took from the car lot's office, trying to get the car to start, the engine coughs, not revving yet.

Behind us, the doors to the library glow with power. They won't last for long. They *don't* last for long. They burn to ash in seconds, falling away from the hinges that hold them like powder to reveal the creature behind them. It steps out into the street, blinking in the light, looking around for us until its eyes fix on us in the car.

Finally, Jack gets the car to start.

The creature lets out another inhuman sound and runs at the car in loping strides, but Jack hits the gas, and even with the layer of ash on the road, he manages to speed away. The creature hits the ground where the car was, clawed hands digging into the road like it's butter.

Kailin Gow

Jack pushes the car to its limit in the next few seconds, so that there's a brief point when I'm sure I see the speed reach ninety. I glance back and see the creature watching, not chasing, obviously having decided that catching us would be too much of an effort.

"It's okay, Jack," I say. "You can slow down."

Jack glances back and slows a little, though he's still doing more than the speed limit would be on a street like this. He doesn't stop until we're well clear of the library. Almost all the way to the freeway.

"That was close," he says. "Too close. Shooting that thing didn't even seem to slow it down."

That obviously bothers him. I don't think Jack likes the idea of an enemy he doesn't know how to kill if he needs to. I know I don't like the idea of an enemy Jack can't kill. If that creature had managed to get hold of us, how long would we have lasted? I don't think it would have been able to burn us, but it still had claws and teeth. It was still too strong to fight.

"Jack, that creature…" I want to avoid this, but I know I can't. We need to talk about it, and we need to do it now. "It burned the doors. It burned whoever that was

35

back there. It has the same powers I do. What does that mean, Jack? Where did it come from?"

Jack shakes his head. "I don't know, Celes."

"Is it connected to me somehow? Am I the same kind of thing it is?" I can feel those questions gnawing away at me. Because if it's something so terrifying and mindlessly evil, what does that make me?

"You're nothing like that thing," Jack says.

"I have the same powers."

"You're nothing like it," Jack repeats, reaching out for me. "You're not a monster, and you never will be."

Trust Jack to guess what's scaring me. How can he know though? How can he know that one day I won't end up like that thing? What if I'm just the first stage on whatever path leads to it?

"You have to trust me, Celes," Jack says. "I don't know what that thing is, but I know you aren't it. You care too much about the world and the people in it. All that cared about was killing."

I nod, knowing that he's right, even though there are still so many doubts nagging at me. "There's so much we don't know," I say. "Where did that creature come

Kailin Gow

from, Jack? Does it have something to do with Hammond?"

"Your guess is as good as mine," Jack says. "It could be up to Hammond. It could be from the future. It could even be something from the past. We don't have enough information to make a guess, except that it seems to have a violent streak."

I think about all the ash in the town. Some of it has to be from the fire that was raining from the sky when we went into the shelter, but how much of it is from that creature, or others like it? How many people has it killed?

"There might be others like it," I say. "There might be dozens of them. Hundreds. There might be whole armies of them."

"Or there might just be a few," Jack says.

I nod. I don't like being like this. Not knowing what's going on. "What we need is more information."

"If we can get it," Jack agrees. "But it isn't the main priority. The priority is to get to Location Thirteen. If we're lucky, the Faders there will know more about what has happened in the past couple of days."

"As well as how to stop those things," I say.

37

Jack nods. "Let's hope so. If there are more of them, then they could potentially wipe out every human out there."

"But we know it doesn't work out like that, don't we?" I say.

Jack shakes his head. "You know we can't take that for granted. We came back to change things, so we have to believe that things can change. If they can, then they can change both ways."

Which means they can get worse as well as better. I've thought about it before. I've thought about it a lot now. We came into the past to try to make things better, but what if we make things worse? What if we've come here to this time to try to save the future, but we actually end up destroying it?

No, we aren't going to allow that to happen. Whatever it takes, we're going to stop the Fever. We're going to save people. We're going to stop creatures like the one we've just run from. First, of course, we need to find a way to do that, but we will. I hope we will at least.

That means getting to Location Thirteen. Jack seems to know that too, because he hits the gas again, heading out onto the freeway and setting off in the direction of Nevada.

FIVE

It's only when we've been on the freeway a little while that I realize we aren't heading south. Instead, we seem to be heading almost due west.

"What's going on, Jack?" I ask. "I thought that we needed to get to Location Thirteen?"

"We do."

"But this isn't the way to the Nevada Desert."

Jack shakes his head. "Not directly, but assuming everything is still there, it's our best shot at getting there quickly."

"Assuming what's still there?" I ask.

Jack smiles. "You'll see."

A half hour later, I do. There's what looks like an old storage facility away to our left, but Jack pulls into it like it's something much more important than that, bringing the car to a halt in front of the imposing looking gates.

40

Kailin Gow

"This is a Location, isn't it?" I guess.

"Not exactly." Jack punches a number into a keypad by the gate, leaning in so that a scanner can identify him. "There aren't any people here. It was never designed as a shelter, or as a place for Faders to work out of. In a way, it's exactly what it looks like. A storage facility."

"But one that stores things for the Underground?" I say. I can see how useful that would be. A place that didn't have to have Faders in it looking after it, but where there would be plenty of things for any Fader who needed them. "What kind of thing do you store here?"

"Just about anything we could think of that a Fader might need in an emergency," Jack says. He smiles again. "Don't worry, you'll get the tour. We're going to need a lot of things for this trip to Nevada."

I look around the place. It's as empty as everywhere else. "Don't you have anyone in these places? I mean, isn't it a security risk just leaving it?"

Jack glances towards a small building by the entrance. "In theory, there should be a couple of local security guards on it who think that it's just a normal storage place. With everything that's going on, I'm not expecting them to be here. There's still plenty of automated security, though."

"What kind of automated security?" I ask.

Jack shrugs. "Pretty basic things near the outside. Alarms, stun plates, that kind of thing. Further in, we're talking automated mini-guns, but it's not like we have a problem there. I have the clearance to go anywhere I want in these units. Or I should..."

He tries the entry pad again. Nothing happens.

"So we're locked out?" I ask.

"I think we should be able to get inside through the office," Jack says. "The question is what's going to happen then. If the power is down for the whole system, then we should be okay, but if there's still emergency power for the inner defenses..."

"Then we could be walking into just about anything," I finish for him.

We go in anyway. We can't afford not to. As Jack said before, we're going to need the contents of this place if we're going to make it to Location Thirteen. If there are dangers inside, then we're just going to have to risk them.

Jack pauses at the door, kissing me.

"What's that for?" I ask.

"Just for being wonderful generally. And because I'm glad I found you again. I'm glad I can remember how much I've always loved you, Celes."

I'm glad of that too, and it hits me then. Jack came back into the past to stop the apocalypse, but I came back just to find Jack. All this way, and I succeeded. I found him, exactly the way I promised myself I would, and apocalypse or no apocalypse, we're together. That's actually pretty impressive, when I think about it like that.

We slip inside the storage facility, and I see that Jack has his gun out. I'm not sure what it will do against automated defense systems, but it's better than nothing. Although I think what's going to keep us safe has more to do with Jack's ability to sense danger. With luck, that will at least keep us from stepping on any shock pads.

"Are you getting anything?" I ask.

Jack shakes his head. "I think the power must be down in the whole facility."

"Well, that's good," I say.

Fever (FADE #4)

"Not really. It means we won't be able to get the front gates open, and for what I came here to pick up, we need the front gates open."

Jack continues to lead the way. I'm not sure I'd trust too many other people to lead me through an abandoned facility like this. Especially not after what we found in the library back in town. Grayson, maybe, but not many others.

We check the facility carefully. Aside from us, it seems to be empty. Jack picks out a door or two, but it seems they aren't locked by the usual arrangement of padlocks that I'd expect in a storage place. Apparently, the Faders prefer automatic doors. Which is as much of a problem as the gate was.

"I can probably burn the doors open," I say.

Jack nods. "I know, but can you get the gate as well? There isn't enough room between the units for what I want."

I think back to what I was able to do at one of the Others' facilities. There, I blew a pretty good hole in one of their base's blast doors.

44

"Maybe. I mean, I can probably make a hole in them."

"A hole won't work," Jack says looking around. How big *is* what he's here to collect? "We need to find a way to open them. There should be a power relay here somewhere. Maybe we'll be lucky and it will just be a blown circuit."

"Which, when we've fixed it, will have mini guns shooting at us," I point out.

"I'm still working on that part," Jack says. I guess that whatever we're here to collect, it must be pretty important. Why else risk our lives over it? "First, we need to find the controls for this place."

That takes us maybe ten minutes. We finally find them in a fenced off area of the storage compound, behind a chain link fence that doesn't take me long to burn through. Behind it, there's a kind of control console, flanked on both sides by what appear to be turrets. I'd thought that Jack might be exaggerating when he mentioned the mini-guns, but here a couple are, right in the perfect position to kill anyone who tries to mess with the system. I'm just glad that they aren't powered up right now.

"So how can we do this?" I ask.

Jack takes a look at the console. It's as dead as the rest of the place. "I think that whatever has been messing with the cars has messed with this too."

"So in theory, I might be able to power it back up with my energy?" I ask.

"Maybe," Jack agrees. He looks at the turrets. "But there's an obvious problem with that. The moment you power it up, those are going to start spinning, and a few seconds after that…"

"We become Swiss cheese."

Jack nods. I look over the console. It looks like there's a security scanner similar to the one on the gate built into it.

"What's this for?" I ask.

"It's so that they can check that anyone trying to use the system isn't an intruder," Jack explains. He looks at it, and I can see him trying to calculate something. "In theory, if I were able to log in, then we'd have complete control over this place, including the defenses. But no, it's too dangerous."

"What's too dangerous?" I ask. "We power the place up, you log in, and then we turn the defenses off. Easy."

"Depending on how long the log in takes," Jack points out. He shakes his head. "Ordinarily, it would be okay. There's a delay deliberately to allow an operator to connect. But we're already trespassing, and we don't know if everything will run at the same speed powered off you, Celes."

"So are you saying we shouldn't do it?" I ask. I look him in the eye. "Is what we're getting here worth it?"

"It could get us to Location Thirteen quickly, and save us all the danger that might be on the way."

"Then it's worth it," I decide, and move up next to the console. "I believe in you, Jack. You can do this. Just be ready to log in when I power things up. On three. One, two... three."

I reach down into myself, pulling up power the same way I did with the car engine. Except this time it can't be just a quick spark. It's a constant stream. One that makes the console hum, and the gears of the turret beside me whir as it comes to life. Slowly, ponderously, it turns towards us, its barrels starting to spin.

"Hurry up, Jack!"

Jack puts his eyes to a scanner, punching in a number on the accompanying keypad at the kind of speeds only he can manage. The mini-gun is spinning faster now, its barrels a rattling whir as they blur their way round and round. Any second now, the first bullets will come out of it to tear the two of us to pieces. What will that be like? Will it even hurt, or will it be so fast that there isn't a chance for it to hurt? I don't want to find out, but it's looking more and more like...

The mini guns stop spinning, turning away from us. There's a grinding noise as the gate at the front of the compound starts to open. Doors around the storage facility raise themselves in near silence.

"You did it!" I say to Jack, stepping away from the console.

"We did it," Jack corrects me. "Come on. Let's go see what there is that can help us."

The first locker we go to contains weaponry. We take a flak jacket each, just in case, while Jack passes me a handgun, a knife, and even a couple of grenades. He's a little more heavily armed by the end of it, with a shotgun strapped to his back and a short, blocky sub-machine gun on a strap.

The weapons aren't the end of it though, because the next locker contains camping supplies. The one after that has food. As for the one after *that*...

"It's a helicopter," I say. "You actually keep a *helicopter* in a storage locker?"

It looks like one of those fast, long range ones the Faders favor. One of the ones we used over Switzerland. Only this one is somehow folded up neatly onto a large steel pallet for moving around. Amazingly, the two of us can move it easily. We take it out to the road in front of the storage location, and in less than another half hour, Jack has it looking like a fully operational helicopter again. We even manage to get extra fuel tanks onto it. We climb in and Jack sets the rotors whirring.

"So," he says through the comm-sets, "was this worth nearly getting shot for?"

Fever (FADE #4)

I nod. "Definitely."

SIX

Jack takes us up into the air effortlessly. Apparently, being in storage has protected the helicopter from whatever afflicted the cars we tried. We have plenty of supplies aboard. Enough to get us to Location Thirteen and maybe beyond, though Jack says it will be sensible to stop and refuel along the way. Neither of us wants to be stranded in the middle of the Nevada Desert with no fuel to get us back out again if there's a problem at Location Thirteen.

I try not to think about that. We're pinning our hopes on help being there. The idea that it might not be, or that the Faders there might have been wiped out as easily as the inhabitants of Washington, just isn't one that we can focus on. Instead, I try looking out at the ground below us as Jack flies the helicopter effortlessly, with the kind of skill that comes from a lot of practice.

Fever (FADE #4)

What I see from up here isn't exactly encouraging though. Down below, the land is a patchwork of scorching, where fire has rained down. We're still low enough that I can see buildings that are little more than burned out shells. Strangely though, others seem intact, and with that small oddity in my mind, I can see that the same is true of the ground below us. Patches of it, even large swathes, are scorched beyond recognition, but other areas are pristine and untouched.

"I hope people were able to make it to shelters," I say. I take a pair of binoculars from the supplies we've brought and look down. "Or that they were at least in the undestroyed areas."

We're close to the White House now. I can see even without the binoculars that it's heavily damaged. Almost destroyed. All that heritage and history, ruined, in just a few short days.

"We need to find a way to talk to any people who are left," I say, knowing that we know more about this crisis than most people do. "We need to be able to tell them how to stay safe, or at least what kind of threats might be out there."

Jack nods and I try the helicopter's radio, but it doesn't seem to be working.

"It's dead," I say. "Do you think everything is like this, Jack?"

"We know that a lot of communications are down," he points out. "The TV in the room didn't last."

I nod. It stayed on long enough to show us Wilson Hammond taking control, but not what happened afterwards. TV, radio, it's like all the ways we used to communicate with one another are just… gone.

"My guess is that the wires and the satellites are damaged," Jack says. "Either fire damage destroyed the connections needed for the systems to work, or…"

"Or?" I ask.

"In theory, solar storm activity could act like an EMP, damaging electronic equipment and causing power surges. And we've just experienced the solar storm to end all solar storms."

I nod. That makes a kind of sense, though it does mean that we're very lucky to have a functioning helicopter. I guess it must up to more than the Faders storing it well. The components must be individually shielded.

"I guess that isn't going to make it so easy to communicate with people," I say.

Jack shrugs and keeps flying. "We'll just have to do it the old fashioned way."

"Face to face?"

"Exactly. Though hopefully we won't need to before we get to Location Thirteen. I don't want to make a bunch of stops beyond those we need for more fuel. The longer we're on the ground, the more chance there is of something going wrong, and I'm not going to risk your safety."

Jack takes the helicopter a little higher then, pushing on south. I keep watching the ground below as the helicopter eats up the miles. Still the ground is that ragged mixture of destruction and perfection, as though someone was trying to burn incomprehensible patterns into the earth below. There's so much destruction that it's hard to comprehend as we fly over towns, villages and open farmland. I guess there's a part of me that hoped that it wasn't really the end of everything, that it was something more local. Something we could avoid if we just went far enough. Well, after an hour we've gone more than a hundred and fifty miles, and the destruction is still there below.

Along with something else.

"Jack, wait!" I call out. "Do you see that?"

"See what?" Jack asks, but he does bring the helicopter to a carefully controlled hover while I point.

"There," I say, as I spot it again. A flash of light, followed by another, the brightness and intensity of the flashes all too familiar. "Did you see it this time, Jack?"

Jack nods. "I saw it. The same as with the creature from the library. There's one down there, and it's burning something."

He doesn't say that it could be someone. He doesn't need to. I don't think I'll ever be able to forget the remains of some poor person left charred beneath that reptilian beast that chased us. I know I won't be able to forget the sight of it coming after us through the library. Sprinting after me while I threw bookcases down in front of it.

"It's okay, Celes," Jack says, obviously guessing what I'm thinking. "It's gone. We got clear."

"But now it's down there," I say. "Or one like it is."

"It has to be another," Jack says. "We're too far away for it to be anything else."

"And is that better?" I demand. "One creature like that is bad enough, but now we know that there are more of them. Even before we get to me."

"To you?" Jack shakes his head. "Don't do this to yourself, Celes."

"Why not?" I look down and see all the destruction there. I see the flashing light that says a creature is killing people. "So much of this is my fault, Jack."

"It isn't your fault, it's Hammond's."

"And who let him live? I did." I shake my head. "We both know that isn't the worst of it though. I've been thinking about it a lot ever since we met the creature, Jack. What if..."

"Don't say it again, Celes," Jack says, cutting me off.

I shake my head. "I *have* to say it. I have to say it because it needs to be said. We need to work out what we're going to do if I end up like one of those creatures. I mean, am I the beginning stages of whatever process creates those things? Or is it worse than that? Do I come from those things? Am I their future form?"

"Are we," Jack corrects me. "Remember, I have some of the same powers."

"I know, Jack. I know."

"And *I* know that you are nothing like those creatures," Jack says. "You aren't one of them. The fact that you have similar abilities... that could be a coincidence."

"You of all people don't believe in coincidences," I say.

"I don't believe that you could ever be one of them either," Jack shoots back.

"And *how* do you know?" I can hear the tension in my voice, and I guess Jack can too. He must know how much the thought of ending up as one of those things scares me.

"I know, because I know what's in your heart." Jack pulls the helicopter around in a tight circle as more flashes come at ground level. "I know that whatever happened, you would never do that."

I don't argue with him. Even though I've already *done* that, I don't argue with him. Maybe Jack just guesses what I'm thinking, because somehow, in the midst of keeping the helicopter under control, he manages to reach out to me.

"Every time you have used your powers, it has been to protect yourself or the people you care about. You've had a good reason."

"And how do we know that the lizard people don't have good reasons, at least by their standards?"

"Lizard people?" Jack raises an eyebrow.

"I have to call them something. And 'lizard people' is a little less scary than 'big, invulnerable thing that nearly killed us'."

"Lizard people it is," Jack agrees.

"You know what really scares me, Jack." It isn't a question.

Jack nods. "I know."

What scares me is that while I've had a good reason for every time I used my power, I could also feel the joy of using it. The dark joy that welled up in me while things, people, burned. There's always a part of me that's horrified by what my power can do, but there's another, deeper, hidden part that seems to revel in it.

I look down at the ground again. "There are people down there, Jack. Every one of those flashes is a person dying."

Jack nods, but he looks torn as he does it. "We might already be too late."

I shake my head. "We can't know that unless we go down there."

"And if we do, then I could be exposing you to danger when I should be getting you safely to Location Thirteen. Everything I've been taught tells me that I should be flying you out of here, Celes. Regrouping with the other Faders. Trying to come up with an effective plan rather than charging in against an enemy we don't have a way to hurt, let alone stop."

Yet he doesn't fly the helicopter out of here. He doesn't move us away from the terrible carnage that must be taking place below. Jack might know what the logic of his mission tells us we should be doing, but he's still a better man than that. I decide to make it easy for him.

"Jack," I say, "we aren't leaving. We aren't just going to abandon people to die."

"Even if it means exposing you to danger? Even if it means that we might not make it to the other Faders in time to warn them about what's going on?"

"My guess is that your uncle and your father are already better informed about what is going on than anyone else," I point out. I shake my head. "Forget Location Thirteen for the moment, Jack. It's a guess. A vague hope. We don't know that there is anyone there, let alone anyone with a solution for all this. But we know that there are people down there, and that they are in trouble. I can't leave them behind, and I think the truth is that you can't either, or you would already have flown us away from all this."

Jack nods. "I guess, if we can help… and maybe it's an opportunity to find out more about those things."

"Maybe," I say, "but the main priority is to get anyone down there out of trouble."

Jack nods, and then smiles to himself.

"What?" I demand. "What's so funny?"

"Not funny," Jack says. "You know before you were asking how I knew you weren't like one of those things? Well, how many of those do you think would stop to help people? Now strap yourself in, we're going down."

SEVEN

Jack takes the helicopter down, not heading directly for the flashes, but close. That's a hard one to judge. We need to be close enough to help, but not so close that we're right on top of any creature like the one that chased us before. In the end, Jack puts us down behind a stand of trees that back onto a small, square, concrete building with a glass front.

As the rotor blades idle, he leaps into the back of the helicopter, grabbing supplies. The submachine gun is just the start. He even grabs grenades. As for me, he throws a spare gun my way, along with a couple of clips of ammunition.

"You know how to use it, right?"

I nod, checking the chamber of the gun before loading and cocking it. I holster it alongside the other pistol Jack gave me. I briefly think about grabbing even more weaponry, but if two pistols aren't going to be enough to keep me safe, I don't know what will do the job.

We hop down from the helicopter, heading around the corner of the building. There are other buildings nearby, set off from the road. They look like office buildings, though the only sign on them is a highly stylized symbol a little like a star in the middle of a series of interlocking rings that remind me a little of the way people draw atoms.

The flashes of light came from here. I'm sure of it. It's just a question of where. There are a few more buildings around us, forming a loose, open compound. In theory, the flashes could have come from any one of them.

"Where…" I begin, but Jack lifts a hand to cut me off. He presses himself flat against the wall of the building, reaching back as he does it to press me to it too. I'm so tight against it that I can feel the roughness of the concrete against the skin of my cheek. Jack is so quiet and focused now, edging forward, the weapon he holds leveled to fire in whatever direction he's looking from moment to moment.

Fever (FADE #4)

A heavy set man in his late fifties rushes from the building opposite us, lumbering across the ground between the buildings. He's wearing a suit and a lab coat, both stained with something darker. Something almost black. What does it say about my life these days that I recognize the blood stain for what it is instantly?

For a moment, I think that Jack might shoot him, he's so ready for action. Certainly he aims at the running man, before pulling his gun down, obviously recognizing that he isn't an immediate threat. Light flashes, and this time, it doesn't come from a creature touching anyone. There's a beam of it, flashing out from the shadows of the building's entrance, missing the running man by inches. He hits the ground in something that seems to be half a dive and half a stumble. Whatever it is, he ends up down in the dirt, scrambling to get to his feet.

He looks terrified, and right then, I guess he has every right to be. Even so, the expression on his face is painful to watch. People shouldn't look that scared of anything. There shouldn't be things in the world capable of doing that to someone. The trouble is, I know exactly the kind of thing that *could* make someone that scared. I've seen them. I've been *chased* by them.

Jack pulls me away from the wall. "Celes, you get him. Make sure that he's safe. I'll..."

"You'll *what* Jack? Take on one of those things on your own?"

Jack shakes his head. "No. I'm not going to do that, but I'm fast enough to cause a distraction and still get away."

"That thing in the library was *fast,* Jack."

He kisses me then, fast and hard. "So am I, and I'm not about to take a risk. I'll see it coming. You know I will. Just focus on this guy. Get him back to the helicopter, or to any other form of transport if that isn't an option. Get to Location Thirteen. Complete the mission."

Why does that sound like Jack saying goodbye?

"Jack..." I start to protest, but he's already moving. He's running, with that better than human speed he has, making his way out towards the building the man has just come from. I can feel my heart beating hard in my chest at the thought of what might be happening there. One heartbeat, then another. I hear the sound of gunfire, and want to run to Jack, but I know he's right. I have to help this man. We landed to help people.

We landed because I talked Jack into it to help people. That thought creeps into me as I start over towards the heavy set man who is only now coming back to his feet. What if Jack is hurt here, or worse? That will be my fault. Even so, I force myself to head over to the man we're trying to help.

"Come on," I say. "Let's get you out of here."

"Thank God, you aren't one of them." He looks bewildered at the fact I'm here, but he lets me take his arm. Close up, he looks haggard, his greying hair a mess, his shirt torn. His dark eyes dart from spot to spot as though expecting an attack at any moment. Maybe he's even right about that.

"One of whom?" I demand.

"Them," he says. "*Them.*"

He points in the direction Jack has run, but I can't see anything there. I can just see how scared this man is. We need to get him clear of this place before he panics.

"Come on," I say. "Let's get you out of here."

He shakes his head. "There's nowhere safe. Our cars..."

"We have transport," I say, pulling him along in one stumbling step, then another. "Is there anyone else here who needs our help?"

"Anyone else?" the question seems almost to take him by surprise. "No. No, they're all... they got them."

"They killed them?" I ask. It's a tough question, and one I don't want to ask someone so obviously terrified, but I know I have to. I can't stand the thought of leaving someone behind.

"They took them. Rounded them up like cattle. I... I was the only one to get away."

"And is there anyone else in any of the other buildings?" I press him.

He shakes his head. "No. I just said. They got all of them. The ones they didn't capture, they... you won't believe me."

"They disintegrated them," I guess.

He nods, and then comes to a halt, looking at me with surprise. "How do you know that?"

67

Fever (FADE #4)

"I know a lot of things," I say, "and it has been a very long day. Now keep moving. Unless you want to be their next victim."

That's harsh and I know it, but Jack is relying on me to get this guy out of there. Worse, the slower he moves, the longer Jack's distraction has to last. That thought is enough to make me practically drag him. He's a big guy, but I'm strong enough to keep him moving easily, keeping him on course for the helicopter. If we can make it back there-

There are more shots, a flash of light from inside the building, shouting. It sounds like there's a full blown battle in there, especially when I hear the dull thud of a grenade detonating. It's loud as it rattles through the building ahead of me, and in that moment, I have only one thought. *Jack*.

The first few shots made sense. The first few shots were his distraction. This isn't a distraction. It can't be. It's more than that. I spin the man with me to face me.

"Listen," I say. "I need to know everything you can tell me about what is going on in there, and I need you to tell me now."

Maybe it's the look on my face, but he doesn't argue. "What do you want to know?"

"What exactly is in there?" I demand. "What is Jack up against? How many, and where in the building are they? What exactly *happened* here?"

He hesitates.

"Tell me!"

"We couldn't predict what would happen!" That comes out as a startled bleat while he raises his hands as though he thinks I might hit him. "We couldn't predict the solar behavior. No one could. We couldn't know what it would do to our equipment, or our experiments."

"What experiments?" I ask. "Who exactly are you?"

"Dr. Troy Florence. I'm a neurologist. My team was doing research that could have helped everyone, but now... they're loose!"

"What's loose?"

Dr. Florence shakes his head. "Not what. Who. We thought we were advancing humanity, but things changed so rapidly. The solar... event must have done something to the experiments."

"Do they look like they're part lizard?" I ask.

69

"No. Nothing like that. They look human. But they aren't. They can do things that no human could ever do. They can manipulate energy in ways that are unbelievable... I know how mad this must sound."

"It doesn't sound mad," I assure him. Or at least no madder than the rest of my life. "Now tell me more."

"Some of them must have been overwhelmed by the effects of the solar energy. They're... insane. Aggressive. They've killed people, and others of their kind. I saw them *burn* people. They burned people with the power of the sun, and I still don't even know how they did it."

"Can they be stopped?" I ask. "Will bullets stop them?"

Dr. Florence looks like he doesn't know how to respond to that. "They're still human. Tougher, stronger... but still human shaped. I *guess* that a bullet would stop one, or maybe several bullets, but you aren't seriously considering..."

I point to the stand of trees. "There's a helicopter hidden behind those trees. On it, you'll find food and supplies. If you know how to use a weapon, you should find those there too." There's more shouting from inside the main building. "Right now, I have to go help the man I love, and if you can't help me, then you need to keep out of the way. Stay on the helicopter until I come, understood?"

Dr. Florence nods. "Who are you?" he asks. "You have helicopters, weapons... are you with the government?"

I think about Wilson Hammond being handed the presidency. Then I think about my own presidency, so far in the future now. "That's pretty complicated. We don't have the time."

"At least tell me your name."

"I'm called Celestra. Celestra Caine. Now go. Head for the helicopter."

He turns to go. I un-holster one of the pistols I got from Jack. I've seen him shoot with one in either hand, but I guess that without practice, this is better. I just hope that it will be enough. No, I can't think like that. I have to believe that this will work.

I sprint over to the main building, not knowing far too many things. I still don't know how many people there are in there, or how dangerous they are. I just know that Jack is in trouble, and I have to help.

EIGHT

I sprint towards the building, my gun coming up as a figure streaks towards me from inside, almost faster than the eye can follow. That figure twists away from my line of fire and a hand comes up to keep the pistol pointed in the other direction. As my reflexes let me think again, I see Jack standing there, looking like he's been in a fight.

"Celes, I thought you were heading to the helicopter? Come on, we need to go. Run."

I start to ask why, but then I see them. They look so ordinary, a man and a woman, with pale, almost grey hair, dressed in dark jumpsuits. They're moving slowly at the moment, and they seem almost like they're asleep, even though their eyes are wide open and staring at us with obvious hatred. There's something about those eyes, too. Something blank and almost empty.

"Go get them," the man says, in a flat monotone.

Fever (FADE #4)

"I am. You get them."

"How about if no one does anything to anyone?" I suggest. I don't raise my gun again, but Jack levels his. "We don't mean you any harm."

The man laughs, taking another step forward. "You think we're going to believe that. We know what you are. Both of you. You're the *things* that burn people up."

"You mean you aren't?" I ask. We saw the flashes from above. Dr. Florence *told* us that people were being burned, yet these two are right. They don't look anything like they might burn things.

"We're not," the woman puts in, "but you are. We can tell. And you have to be stopped."

I raise my gun. "I don't want to hurt you, but if you come any closer, I'll shoot. Now, who are you? What are you?"

"*You're* asking *us*?" the man demands. He looks at the woman, like it's some kind of joke I don't get.

"Who are you?" I repeat.

"Celes," Jack says, interrupting. "There's no time to talk. Things are getting too dangerous here."

"You've *seen* something?"

74

Jack nods tightly. "We need to get out of here. We need to leave *now*."

I hear the urgency in his voice and start to back away, but it's too late. I hear the whir of rotor blades, and a second later a large, black helicopter with multiple weapon systems hanging from it is hovering over the compound. A voice booms from it, amplified through speakers. It's unmistakable. Wilson Hammond speaks down to us, his voice carrying easily over the whole space.

"Celes. Jack. There you are. I was starting to wonder where you might have gone after you escaped my shelter. It's good to see that you got through the apocalypse okay. Of course, you might not like what happens next so much, but it isn't like I care what you think. Good work in finding them, you two."

That's obviously directed at the man and the woman on the ground. They work for Hammond? The woman takes a step forward and I kick her back.

"Run!" Jack yells.

We do, but with the helicopter hanging over us, we don't dare run for our own transport. Instead, we sprint with Jack firing seemingly blind behind us, heading for the nearest of the buildings, the one with the largely glass front. There's a roar above us and the ground nearby is churned up by gunfire. The helicopter is attacking!

We sprint for the safety of the building, and I find myself wondering if it really will be safe. What if Wilson Hammond's helicopter has rockets? What if we go in there and he brings the building down around us? I'm still thinking that when Jack shoves me through the door, turning to send a burst of gunfire back at the helicopter.

He jams the door shut and reaches forward to pluck a grenade from my belt. With him so close, it's easy to think about him doing so many other things, and I find myself wondering how I can think that way about him even in the middle of being attacked?

Jack pulls the pin on the grenade, wedging it into the door handle, then he takes me by the arm, pulling me deeper into the building, down empty corridors.

"We need to get away from here before they decide to break in."

We move into a room that looks the same as any of the others from the outside. Inside, this one has overturned tables and chairs, a selection of shattered

76

glassware that was probably used in experiments, and a few noticeboards with information about safety procedures. I wonder if they have anything suitable for *this*? There's also a small window in one corner, obviously there to let in more light.

There's a boom somewhere behind us. Jack's grenade trap going off.

"Has it-" I begin, but Jack puts a finger to my lips, pulling me down behind the nearest of the upturned tables. He's just in time. I can hear footsteps approaching, and angry voices. The man and the woman from before.

"We'll get them," the man says. "Now that we know who they are, they aren't getting away. Even if they do, they'll be public enemy number one."

"We have to find them first," the woman replies. "Find them and take them down without them burning us. Honestly, I don't see why *things* like that get to live."

"They don't," the man points out, and I hear him working the slide on a gun. "Not much longer at least."

"Yes, yes. Very macho, but where exactly do you think they're going to be?"

"We'd find them if you'd shut up."

Fever (FADE #4)

Maybe it's the fact that I have to stay still through all of this, but I find myself concentrating more and more on just how uncomfortable it is, being stuck down behind a table. I know I can't move, but crouching here, it's hard to do anything else. I shift slightly, not much, just enough so that I can see them, because I can't stay still *and* not see people who might be out to kill me.

I find myself staring straight into the dead eyes of the woman.

"There! They're *there*! What are you waiting for?"

Jack's on his feet in an instant, sending a burst of automatic fire in their direction. Shots fly back at us, punching holes in the table, sending shards of wood flying.

"This isn't good cover," Jack says, pulling me deeper into the room, behind more tables and chairs. "Bullets go through wood. Even with it concealing us, eventually…"

More shots ring out, punctuating his point. Jack returns fire. I do the same, not able to see where I'm aiming, but anything that makes these people keep back from the doorway has to be a good thing.

"We're boxed in," Jack says.

I shake my head, pointing silently to the window in the corner. It's a little off the ground, but if we grab one of the overturned desks to stand on, it should give us another way out. The only problem is that anyone climbing through it is going to be pretty exposed.

Jack nods. "Okay," he says. "I'll cover your escape. Make it to the helicopter and don't look back."

I slap his arm. "Why is that *always* your answer to situations like this? Are you trying to get rid of me?"

"Celes..."

"I'm serious, Jack. We both go or we don't go at all."

"How?" Jack shoots back, while simultaneously... well, shooting back.

I point to the door. "Do you think they're going to want to walk into another grenade trap? Come on, we need to push them back to the door."

"Celes." Jack's voice drops to a whisper. "We don't have any more grenades with us. Unless you have one?"

"The point is that they don't *know* that," I whisper back. "If we can close the door, what do you think they're going to think?"

79

Fever (FADE #4)

Jack nods and grabs hold of the nearest table. I grab it with him and we shoot over the top, forcing our way forward. It isn't much of a shield, but I guess it's mostly a question of having *something* between us and the bullets heading our way, just so that we can bring ourselves to keep moving forward. I fire whenever I see a hand or a head sticking out around the cover of the door.

Jack reaches out, grabbing the door and slamming it shut. He wedges it with a chair while I grab another, clambering up onto a table to smash the window. I try to get as much of the glass as I can, but even so, I know it isn't going to be comfortable climbing through it.

"Get through," I tell Jack, on the basis that he's bigger than me. If he won't fit, then we'll have to find another way. Maybe I can blow a hole in the wall with my power. It looks like I don't have to though because Jack is up on the table in two running steps, leaping through smoothly. "Show off."

I climb through more cautiously, turning and firing back as I hear the door give way. Jack pulls me through the window, then lifts his submachine gun high to spray the room with bullets.

"Run!" he yells. I don't need him to tell me twice. The trees are just a little way away, and we run for them, putting them between us and the bullets that start to come fizzing past us.

"We need to get to the helicopter!" I yell, pausing to fire back through the trees. Hopefully, the two trying to kill us won't be too quick to follow if they think that there are bullets headed their way.

We run from tree to tree, while ahead of us I can hear the sound of rotor blades spinning up to speed. I think of Dr. Florence in the helicopter. Does he know how to fly one? I hope not, because if he does, Jack and I are about to be stranded.

We run for the helicopter, making it there while the scientist is wrestling with the controls, trying to make something happen. I leap into the back, while Jack shoves Dr. Florence aside in the driver's seat.

"Sorry, but we don't have enough time for you to learn to fly. Strap in, because here we go. I just hope Hammond got bored with that helicopter of his."

I strap myself in quickly, grabbing more ammunition while I do it and reloading my gun. I fire as figures start to appear on the edge of the trees. Then we're airborne, and we don't have to worry about them anymore. Just about attack choppers. Thankfully though, there doesn't seem to be any sign of Hammond's.

"I'm sorry," Dr. Florence says, "I was just so frightened..."

"You were lucky," I say. "Do you even know how to fly a helicopter?"

The scientist shakes his head.

"Look at what Jack has to do to work it. Three sets of controls. If you'd gotten off the ground, you would have crashed."

"Yes," Dr. Florence says, suddenly flustered. "I see. I... I'm sorry."

"That doesn't matter now," Jack says. "What matters is that we continue on to Location Thirteen."

I nod, and we start on our way. And if there's a black speck on the very edge of the horizon, I don't pay it much attention.

NINE

Jack gets us clear of the facility, continuing on our original course. He flies that way for hours, putting ground between us and the site of our last battle. Eventually, he must feel safe, because he flicks a few switches before turning to me and gesturing to the controls.

"Take over, Celes. I want to talk to Dr. Florence."

"Take over?" I say. "I don't know how to fly a helicopter."

"Just keep the controls steady," Jack says, clambering out of his seat.

I take his place, even though I'm not sure that this is such a good idea. As the controls fit into my hands though, I realize that I *do* know what to do. Memory floods back into me, and I remember flying myself in the future, piloting everything from small transport copters to full attack ones. Anything that would let me get to where my presidential duties needed me.

Fever (FADE #4)

So I hold the controls steady, which is probably just as well, because a second later, Jack has a grip on Dr. Florence's shirt, holding him half out of the door of the helicopter.

"What are you doing?" the scientist complains.

"I'm finding out the truth." Jack says it perfectly calmly, like threatening to drop someone out of a helicopter is perfectly normal for him. "Now talk. What was that place. What's your connection to Wilson Hammond? Why did he suddenly show up?"

"Please," Dr. Florence says, sounding terrified, "I'll tell you anything you want to know, just pull me back in."

Jack hauls him back inside. "Talk."

"Please, I'm just a researcher. That's what that place was. An R&D space for Hammond Industries."

"So you did the research that came up with his heat resistant materials?" I ask.

"More than that." Dr. Florence suddenly looks pretty nervous, even considering that he's just been held out of a helicopter. "Much more."

84

"Like what?" Jack demands. "And who were those people chasing after you? They looked pretty weird, but they didn't have any abilities that I could see."

"Abilities? You mean like burning?" Dr. Florence shakes his head. "No, they aren't the ones who can do that."

"Then who were they?" Jack repeats.

"They're Hammond's people. I guess I am too. Or I was. I was his chief researcher. We did the materials research you're talking about. We worked from a specimen with those abilities to create exactly what we needed."

"A specimen?" I ask from the front of the chopper. "You're talking about someone like me and Jack? Someone from the future?"

"No," Dr. Florence says, and his eyes widen in surprise as he says it. "You two… you're from the future? How is that possible?"

"Never mind that," Jack says, looking slightly annoyed. Have I done the wrong thing by mentioning the future? Maybe I have. After all the point of an

85

interrogation is to get information out of the other person, not to tell them more.

"You mentioned specimens," Jack continues. "Were these specimens people?"

Dr. Florence hesitates, and I see Jack start to move again. "Yes," Florence says. "They were people. People who suffered brain seizures. We were trying to find a treatment for them, but also to learn more about the way the brain works. We learn more about the way the body works when there is something going wrong, you know."

"Tell us about what you did," I say. "How did these people become 'specimens'?"

"We called them our experiments," Hammond says. "We were trying experimental treatments. Things we thought might help. Hammond wanted to test new drugs on them. When the solar event happened though, something changed in them. They were able to absorb the sun's energy and use it in ways that were just... incredible. Ordinarily, we had them come in for a day at a time for testing, but then Hammond wanted to round them up. Keep them there by force."

"Why did he want to do that?" I ask.

"He said something about wanting to test these 'new ones' against the 'ones from the future'. No one knew what he was talking about, but by then, with everything that happened… most of us didn't dare to do anything other than what we were told."

"So how did you survive unscathed?" Jack asked.

"The lab is built to withstand just about anything," Dr. Florence explained. "It was designed with the possibility of dangerous tests from the start."

"Or as a shelter," I suggest.

"He had us add the new materials to it as we came up with them," Dr. Florence added.

"So," Jack says, "if you were working so closely with Hammond, why were his people after you?"

"Because after our test subjects changed, I didn't want to do the things to them that he demanded. I signed up to try to help people, not to lock them away and test them to destruction. The man's insane. Inhuman."

"Maybe he isn't human," Jack mutters. I find myself thinking of the way Hammond was before the apocalypse, and I think I agree with him.

"What exactly did he want you to do?" I ask.

Fever (FADE #4)

"He provided a serum that he said would neutralize the more dangerous aspects of the test subjects, returning them to normal, but it was clear from my preliminary tests that the dosages he stipulated would kill them. Yet he insisted that they should be given the full doses."

"He wanted to kill them?" I say.

"Why would he do that?" Jack demands. "It doesn't make sense."

Dr. Florence shrugs. "He said that he didn't want their 'condition' to spread. He said that they were dangerous. Yet he didn't even consider other options."

"What kind of other options?" I ask.

"These people are still human," Dr. Florence says. "Still thinking, feeling beings. Yes, their condition makes them angry and powerful, but surely that just means that we have to find a way to manage it? We don't kill people when they can't control their actions. It isn't right."

I nod and happen to look out at the horizon, where ahead, the desert is starting to open out. Something catches my eye.

"Jack? Come on up here."

Jack nods. "I'll be right there. Dr. Florence, if what you say is true, you might be exactly what we're looking for. You'd better hope you aren't lying."

"I'm not," Dr. Florence assures him.

Jack comes up to join me. "What can you see?"

I nod out to where a large rock formation is rising from the floor of the desert. It consists of spurs of rock, surrounding a central, flat topped hill almost big enough to call a mountain. There's no sign of damage on it from the fire. There *is*, however, the gleam of metal somewhere below. "I know Locations all look different, but that certainly looks odd enough to me."

Jack smiles, and some of the tension leaves his eyes. "For a non-Fader, you've got a good eye. That's Location Thirteen. Those rock spurs hide a way into natural caverns. The central one has ancient ice at its heart, providing natural cooling. Come on, let's head down."

He takes the controls from me gently and gets ready to bring the chopper down, yet as he does, I look out of the window again. There's a black speck on the horizon. The same black speck that was there before.

89

"Jack, wait!"

"What is it?" Jack asks.

I point and he turns our helicopter to get a better look. Jack gasps.

"It's Hammond's chopper. He's followed us."

"But how?" I ask. I look at the dials and instruments of our helicopter. Sure enough, there's radar spinning in the center. "Shouldn't we have picked him up?"

Jack shakes his head. "Helicopters have a pretty small profile anyway, and if his is using stealth technology... why didn't we spot this, Celes?"

The truth is that we *did* spot him, back at the lab. It's just that his helicopter was far enough away not to seem like anything important. It was only seeing it again that made it seem significant. Like so many other things, it's only now that it's too late that it makes sense.

"I guess we weren't expecting him to follow us," I say. That's true too. Wilson Hammond was quick to attack us back at his lab. He even sent in his two thugs to finish the job. So it would have made more sense for him to come after us with all guns blazing than to simply shadow us from a distance.

Except that it's obvious now what his plan was. Panic us. Make us run. *Keep* us running until we led him straight to Location Thirteen. Which we have. Or at least, which we'll have led him to if we let him know that it's here.

"We have to lose him, Jack," I say. "We have to keep going and pretend that this place has nothing to do with us, then we have to leave him behind and double back."

"That will be hard if Hammond has radar too," Jack says. And he will. An attack helicopter like that *has* to have it. "Unless..."

"Yes?" I say.

"I think I see a way that might work. Strap yourself in, Celes, and tell the doctor to do the same."

I go back and give Dr. Florence Jack's instructions. The scientist looks a little worried, though apparently the thought of Wilson Hammond catching up to him scares him more. He straps himself in. I strap myself in beside Jack, waiting to see what he'll do.

Fever (FADE #4)

For a while, he doesn't do anything, just heading deeper into the desert, out over more rocky outcrops, stands of cacti, even lusher patches with woodland and water running through them. It's only when we're well clear of Location Thirteen that he dives. He plunges the helicopter behind an outcrop, using the shadow of it as a natural block on Hammond's instruments. He takes it in a tight turn around the other side, staying low to the ground.

Still, the black helicopter is there. It's closer now, obviously worried by the sudden maneuvers, but we haven't lost it yet. Instead, it slots in behind us as Jack races along the desert floor, kicking up dust with the rotor blades as we pass.

"It isn't working," he says. "But we *have* to lose them. If they get to Location Thirteen, they'll find every Fader who survived the apocalypse. We can't allow that. Whatever it takes, we have to protect the others."

"Then let's find out what this helicopter can do," I suggest.

"Are you saying we should outrun them?"

"I'm saying we should *outlast* them. Are attack helicopters made for long distance work?"

Jack shakes his head. "But when they realize what we're doing, they might shoot us down."

"Then we'll just have to make ourselves into a harder target to catch," I suggest.

Jack nods. "I can do that."

He flips a switch, and the helicopter roars forward.

TEN

"Hold on tight!" Jack calls out, before pushing the speed of our helicopter up to its maximum. I'd thought that this wouldn't be able to go too fast, since it's designed for long range transport, but apparently, it has some good pace too. The ground below us blurs past. And I can see the ground, because Jack plunges us towards it.

"Jack-" I start to say, but he shakes his head.

"The only way we'll lose them is if we make them dodge. Trust me, Celes. I know what I'm doing. Now look back and see if you can spot them. If they aren't following us, then I could be giving them a straight shot down at our rotor blades."

That sounds bad. I glance back, trying to spot Hammond's helicopter and make sure that it isn't doing exactly that. For a moment, I can't see it, and I start to worry that maybe it's doing exactly what Jack just said. I look up trying to see it above us, can't see it there either, then glance back again.

It's right there behind us, closer now than it was. Worse, I can see the mini-guns on its outside rotating, spitting fire as bullets fly from them. With the noise of our rotor blades, I can't hear their roar, but I find myself bracing for the impact of the bullets. Only when Jack pulls us sharply sideways do I breathe a sigh of relief.

He keeps us dodging, flying dangerously low now, heading for rocky outcrops and skimming the tops of cacti as we fly past. He ducks us into a ravine, Hammond's helicopter following us down into it with another burst of firepower. There's less room to dodge here. There's less room for Jack to do anything except concentrate on navigating the ravine's twists and turns without crashing.

I realize then that's probably Jack's plan. He keeps our helicopter low, almost skimming the ravine's floor and jerking it around the tightest of corners with the kind of ease someone might get from flying them plenty of times before. Yet with Jack, that isn't how he's managing it. He's picked the one environment for this chase where he *knows* his short term visions of the future will give him an advantage. Wilson Hammond's helicopter has to risk crashing at every turn to keep up, and if he loses sight of us once, we'll be away while his radar is still blocked by the walls of the canyon. It's a clever move. Exactly the kind of move only Jack would make.

Yet somehow, Hammond's attack chopper *is* keeping up. Maybe it's because, no matter how fast our helicopter is, it isn't designed for flat out speed. Though it does seem to have one or two extra tricks. A warning light flashes in the cockpit, alarms sounding. I look back to see a flaming streak that can only be a missile heading towards us. Yet a second later, it explodes as Jack presses a button on our helicopter's controls.

"Chaff countermeasures," he explains, pulling the helicopter into a screeching climb as ahead of us, the canyon's end wall looms large. For a moment, all I can see is the bright blue of the sky, while the sheer force of gravity presses me hard back into my seat until I can barely breathe.

He levels out, and Hammond's helicopter is still behind us. A little further back, but still behind us. Jack pushes the pace still further, skimming through a gap between two rock formations that barely looks big enough for our helicopter. He forces the chase on, drawing it out, obviously trying to test the fuel capacity of the helicopter behind us.

Then suddenly, I spot another canyon. One that seems almost to cut a river in half. No, it's two rivers, pouring into it so that dual waterfalls flow and foam down into the canyon valley below. I point to it. "There, Jack."

Jack nods, plunging us down towards it, heading for the waterfalls. For a moment, I think that he's misjudged it. That it's too much even for reflexes with his extra warning. For that moment, all I can see is the spray of the water, the mist from the waterfalls rising around us, their roar even louder than our helicopter.

Then Jack jerks his controls sideways, pulls on them again, and we're stationary. I try to make sense of it, looking around while beside me, Jack balances the helicopters controls in a constant dance with the air around us. Ahead, I can see a falling sheet of water, rainbows running through it as the light strikes it, while beside us, there is only rock.

Fever (FADE #4)

He's pulled the helicopter in behind the waterfall. *Behind* it. He's controlling it there, beneath a natural overhang he couldn't have seen coming down. Only someone with his talents could possibly have done this, and even then, it's a feat of flying that's kind of hard to believe. Maybe that's the point though, because I see something large and dark flash by beyond the wall of water. Even Hammond, it seems, can't believe that we could possibly be here.

Time passes. How much, I'm not sure, because things are too tense in the cockpit of the helicopter to risk checking. Jack is making constant small adjustments to the helicopter, holding it there beneath the overhang, but how long can he keep that up for? Worse, what if Hammond spots us? In a space like this, we'd be trapped. How long do we dare wait?

Eventually, Jack eases the helicopter forward, out of the shelter of the waterfall. It gives me a good view of the valley beyond. It's beautiful. Where the rest of the land around us is parched and dry, the combination of these two small rivers has made this canyon lush and green. It's tree filled and wet, a lost oasis of greenery in the middle of otherwise empty lands.

Jack takes the helicopter up to the level of the canyon lip, obviously looking around for Wilson Hammond's attack chopper. There's no sign of it. Obviously, it has either headed off in search of us elsewhere, or it ran out of fuel for the chase. Even so, we stay low, trying to keep from being easily identifiable on radar.

That makes the journey back to Location Thirteen slow going. Especially when it starts to get darker. Jack has to take the helicopter up further when that happens, just to keep us from crashing. He flies on the instruments then, using them to plot our course heading and keeping us moving until I can see a strange, slightly eerie green light in the distance.

"The Faders will have coated some of the rock floor near the base with luminous paint," Jack explains. "It's not enough to let someone pick out Location Thirteen if they don't know roughly where it is, but once they do, it can lead them in."

Fever (FADE #4)

Jack focusses on it, taking us towards it. There really isn't much of a glow there. I guess that if I didn't know what it was, I'd think that it was something natural. Strange, but natural. Jack brings our helicopter directly over it, bringing us down slowly. I wonder if people inside Location Thirteen know that we're there? They must, mustn't they? I can't imagine Faders who don't want to know when people are getting too close to their bases.

Jack's touch down is perfect. I barely feel it. In the dark, working purely by the helicopter's dials and readouts, that's pretty impressive. Not as impressive as hiding us beneath a waterfall, maybe, but still impressive. The rotors whir to a halt, and I jump out of the helicopter, looking around. Thanks to my abilities, I don't have a problem with the dark.

I reach back into the helicopter, grabbing some of the bags from inside. Dr. Florence is still there, looking around and apparently not seeing much. I grab a flashlight and throw it to him. Jack is busy grabbing branches from the closest tree, pulling out camouflage netting from within the helicopter and pulling it over it.

100

He steps inside, helping me to unload bags. No one has come out from Location Thirteen. Either they don't know we're here, or they're simply waiting for us to come in. Maybe they don't feel like sending out a welcoming committee to help with the bags. Talking of which, Jack throws a couple of bags at Dr. Florence, who catches them inexpertly. I think he's just trying to spread the load, but then I realize that it's a move that leaves Jack's hands free.

He takes Dr. Florence by the arm. "There isn't enough time for me to run all the tests on you that I'd like to," Jack says, "but you'd better believe that until I'm certain about exactly who you are, I'll be watching you."

Dr. Florence nods. "I understand."

I don't say anything. I know Jack likes to be careful. Besides, if his instincts are telling him that we *need* to be that careful, then maybe I should listen to them.

We set off walking through the dark, down to what appears at first to be nothing more than a natural fissure in the rock. We step through one at a time. It's colder inside, and it gets colder still as we make our way along what turns out to be a passageway heading deep into the rock. That passageway twists and turns before finally stopping dead at a heavy steel door. There's a surprisingly old fashioned looking key hole in it.

"I hope you have a key," I say to Jack.

"Every Fader has the key," Jack assures me, and puts his finger in the key hole. I realize then that it must be one of the fancy biometric locks the Faders love so much. "The key hole is just in case someone wanders in by accident. They just think it's an old storage room, or a mine, or something. They don't see the level of technology that's here."

The door grinds back slowly, revealing a brightly lit corridor beyond, with a trio of elevators lined up on one side. Jack pushes a button to call the middle one. Throughout all this, Dr. Florence is staring at everything like he can't quite believe it.

"What is all this? Another research facility? Those materials on the walls… I thought you weren't anything to do with Hammond?"

"We aren't," I assure him. "Trust me, once you've met more Faders, you'll understand."

Jack nods as the elevator doors open, pushing Dr. Florence inside. "If you're lucky, you might even get to remember what you learn. Welcome to Location Thirteen, Doctor."

I step into the elevator beside Jack and Dr. Florence. The doors slide shut without a sound, its bright lights completely at odds with the entrance to the Location. Jack pushes another button on the elevator controls, and slowly, smoothly, we start to move down into the depths of Location Thirteen.

ELEVEN

The door to the elevator slides open as it comes to a halt, revealing a large, open room with screens flashing up data around the edges. It looks so much like the blank room in Location Six that I first saw so long ago. It's a high-tech, efficient kind of place, so different from the farmhouse of Location Four, or the manor house of Location Two.

There are people seated all around the room, including a clutch of men seated in front of one of the panels on the walls, obviously monitoring things on the outside. Jack starts to make his way over, pulling Dr. Florence with him. The scientist looks more than a little reluctant to move any further into one of the Underground's Locations, but Jack doesn't exactly give him a choice.

The men Jack goes over to are all obviously Faders, dressed in dark suits and with that slight edge of wariness to their movements that I've learned to recognize around them. Plus we're in a Location, so what else would they be? There are five of them, all in their twenties and early thirties. One looks round as Jack approaches, leaping up to give him a guy hug.

"Jack! It's great to see you, mate!" His accent is broad Australian, and so are those of the other four as one by one they stand to welcome Jack. All of them look to be in good shape, and I don't mean that just in terms of how athletic they look. They're all free from any signs of sun damage or any other injuries from the apocalypse. I guess they've been pretty lucky.

They're all friendly enough, inviting us to come and sit with them, yet I don't know any of them. In fact there aren't any familiar faces in the room. Not even the one face I was really hoping to see. Grayson isn't here. At least, he isn't in this room. But if he heard we were coming, surely he would have been here?

I don't have much time to think about that though, because Jack is busy introducing us all.

"Celes, these are the guys from Location Nine, out near Melbourne. They only just survived to make it here when their Location was destroyed."

"Completely burned," one of them says, moving forward to greet me. He's in his mid-twenties, with short blond hair and sparkling blue eyes. There's something about him that makes it easy to imagine him surfing off an Australian beach. "The whole Location is gone."

"It sounds like the five of you must have seen quite a bit," Jack says.

The other man, who seems to be the leader of the Australians there, nods. "The ride over was fun. Jim-o had to repair the chopper in the middle of the desert. What about you? Where were you when it happened?"

Jack looks over at me, and I can guess what he's thinking. We can't tell them about our real mission, from the future. Even if he trusts these men, it would still cause too many complications for it to be a good idea.

"We were in a shelter," he says instead. He puts an arm around me. "Guys, this is Celestra Caine."

The blond haired guy holds out a hand for me to shake. "Nice to meet you, Celestra. I'm Niall. That's Joseph, Vincent, Jim, and Ray."

They greet me with a mixture of open friendliness and obvious curiosity. "How did you hook up with Jack?" Vincent asks me.

It's another question where I can't give them the whole truth. "Jack was assigned to protect me, but after that things kind of spiraled out of control a little. We're working together these days. Tell me more about Location Nine."

"There's not a lot to tell," Niall says. "It was a nice place outside the city. Good sheep country. We reckon we probably caught the first of the solar flares and the fires. Well, it's dry enough for bush fires at the best of times, but this was worse."

"How bad was it?" I ask. I know it's not an easy subject to talk about, but we need to know if we're going to understand the scale of the destruction Wilson Hammond has brought to the world. We need to know what kind of support is going to be out there when it comes to rebuilding. There's another reason I want to know, too. I didn't see the destruction, locked up in Wilson Hammond's shelter. I don't know what it was like for people caught out in it.

People like Grayson. People like my Faded family, out there somewhere with no memory of me.

"There were thirty of us at Location Nine," Niall says. He looks around at the others. "These guys are what's left."

I can feel a leaden sensation in my stomach just hearing that. "I'm sorry."

Niall shrugged. "Don't be. We made it. That's what's important. If it weren't for some of the stuff Dr. Cook gave us to add to our place, we'd all be dead." He nods to Jack. "We're lucky to be working for him. At least he was prepared for this."

"Do you know where he is?" Jack asks. "Celestra and I have been looking for him, and for some of the other Faders."

"He should be here somewhere," Niall says, and in that moment, panels at the other side of the room slide back to reveal Sebastian Cook. He's still well dressed, but he looks a little leaner than he did before, and a lot more

108

tired. It looks like the apocalypse has really taken it out of Jack's father.

"Jack! I heard that you were here, but I wanted to see it with my own eyes." He rushes forward, enfolding Jack in a hug. Just for the briefest of moments, Jack looks like he has tears in his eyes. I guess that no one else spots that though.

Jack pulls back, obviously remembering the formality they maintain while they're working. He holds out a hand. "Dr. Cook. It's good to see that you're well."

Sebastian just pulls him into another hug. "There's no need for formalities now, Son. I thought I'd lost you. Everyone here knows that you're my son."

Actually, things are more complicated than that, thanks to the mechanics of time travel. Jack is Sebastian's son, but at the same time, he is a clone of himself from the future. I guess none of that makes Sebastian love his son any less.

"I'm glad you're all right, Dad," Jack says when they pull back. His expression grows a little more serious. "Celes and I were kept in a shelter, hidden from the outside. Can you fill us in on the details of everything that has happened in the last few days?"

"There's a lot to tell, Jack," Sebastian says. "A lot of it, we don't even know yet, because the details haven't come in. We've taken every signal we can get hold of, grabbed reports from stragglers and tried to piece things together as best we can, but still, the picture is pretty incomplete at the moment."

"What *do* you know?" I ask.

Sebastian looks at me. It occurs to me that most of his memories of me will still be of a frightened girl he was trying to help. Even so, I think I've proved myself enough by now to deserve an answer.

Sebastian seems to think so too. "We think that somewhere in the region of two thirds of the world's population is gone."

"Gone? You mean dead?"

Sebastian nods. "Urban areas seem to have been hit hardest. Mexico City, Kolkata, Beijing... there doesn't seem to be much left of them after the fire storms. And even where people survived those... there are reports of disease. It could just be the breakdown in sanitation systems now that there isn't anyone to maintain them, but..."

"It isn't," I say. I can remember sitting in my office, watching the archived accounts of the apocalypse. Watching people die. The fire was terrible, but the plagues were worse. I can remember forcing myself to watch because I wanted to tell myself what was at stake. What we had to change.

Yet it's happening. Everything we tried to do to change things, and it's still happening. There's something so helpless about that. Like what we do counts for nothing. Yet I can't believe that. Not unless I'm willing to abandon my world to its destruction. Not unless I'm willing to stand by while billions of people die from the plague phases of the apocalypse.

"Where's Johnny?" I ask.

"The kid?"

There isn't enough time for me to explain, and in any case, explaining would also mean explaining my mission in front of a room full of strangers. Yet right now, in this instant, Johnny seems like the only person who can help. Okay, so he couldn't cure the Fever, but the advances he made in medical science even on top of what we gained over a thousand years of progress mean that he should be able to deal with *this*. If anyone can, at least.

"Where is he?" I ask again. "Did we get him back? Is he okay?"

Sebastian shakes his head solemnly.

"He's not... dead?" I don't know what we'll do if Johnny is dead. I can remember snatches of things, ideas about how our medicine works in the future, but I don't know the detail. I'm not a doctor. I don't have enough to recreate any of it.

"He's not dead," Sebastian says, "but he *is* hurt. He was on his way to Location Ten, but the helicopter he was on didn't make it. They had to detour when the solar storm came. They headed this way, thankfully, and we were able to get him inside, but they took some pretty serious hits on the way. I guess as a kid, Johnny wasn't able to take that as well as some of the others."

How badly is he hurt? I don't ask it aloud, because there are too many details about Johnny that I don't want to go into here, with strangers nearby. It's not that I don't

112

trust them, particularly if Jack trusts them, but I've been wrong before.

"He's here then?" I ask.

Sebastian nods.

"Then I need to see him," I say.

"He's pretty beaten up right now," Sebastian says, but I know it can't be that bad. If *anyone* knows how to keep themselves in one piece, it's Johnny, after all. "He keeps insisting that we should let him treat himself, rather than leaving it to the experts."

"Then you should probably have listened to him," I say. "Now, quickly, we need to see him if we're going to have a chance of doing something about all this."

Sebastian looks to Jack and then nods. "Okay, he's down in the cave with the others. We'll go see them now if you want."

"I do," I say, starting to follow him. I just hope that I'm right, and Johnny can do everything I remember. Maybe *this* time we can save more of the world.

Fever (FADE #4)

TWELVE

Sebastian leads us to another elevator. The doors close in front of us silently, and again, there's the sensation of movement. It occurs to me that this Location has more power left than most of the towns I've seen. By now, I'm starting to lose track of where we are in the rock that we saw from outside. When the doors swing open, it's cold. Cold enough that I'm grateful for the warm coats that are on a rack by the elevator doors.

The reason for that cold is obvious from the moment I set foot in there. Somehow, impossibly, the interior of the space we're in is coated in ice. It shines as light from above cascades down on it, reflecting and refracting, spinning different colors with every new facet of itself. There are planes and crags of it around the walls, with parts of it worked smooth, while others are ragged and shifting.

"How is there ice in a desert?" I ask.

Fever (FADE #4)

"This ice is old," Sebastian explains. He moves around the walls, almost touching it, but not quite. He does go to a computer station, tapping in a few things. "We're not sure how it would have formed, perhaps it's a hangover from the last ice age, but once it did, the lower temperature in this cavern would have helped sustain it. Now, it's so thick and so old that it would take decades to melt, even if we weren't careful with the temperature. It was like working with rock, when we dug this out."

"It's beautiful," I say. It is. It's almost like being surrounded by diamonds. Better, because diamonds are just cold and dead, while the water that's at the heart of the ice is what life needs.

"Beautiful, but also useful," Sebastian explains, while I follow along with Jack and Dr. Florence bringing up the rear. "Ordinarily, we use it to keep the temperatures in here low enough to use supercomputers in our work, but recently, it proved to be a very effective defense against the fire storm."

"But that..." I try to think. "I know you were putting in heat shielding after Jack and I warned you about what might be coming, but for a place like this, you would have already have to have known."

Sebastian shakes his head. "We just made use of the resources that were already available to us. Trust me, we were lucky to be able to do this much. The only people who were able to prepare for the apocalypse were those who had a hand in creating it. Weren't they, Dr. Florence? Or did you think I wouldn't look up who my son was bringing in?"

He looks over at the scientist, and it's obvious that Sebastian has at least some idea of who the man is. Dr. Florence puts up his hands like he thinks Sebastian might pull out a gun and shoot him. The scientist seems to be so scared of everything right now. But then, he's had a lot to be scared of. And if it turns out that he knew, he will have again.

"Please, I didn't know. I swear. If I'd known what Hammond was doing, and how it would hurt so many people, I would never have gone along with it. I would have told someone. I would have tried to stop him."

Somehow, I doubt that Dr. Florence would have had the guts for that. Though he did say no to Hammond

117

enough for his thugs to want to kill him. Maybe I've misjudged him. Maybe I just don't know enough to judge him. After all, how much of him have I really seen in the past few hours?

"I don't think anyone knew," Dr. Florence says. "Just his staff and maybe a few of his closest advisors."

Like his chief researcher? I don't say that though. It would only make things more difficult. I don't know what to make of Dr. Florence. I don't know whether to trust him or not. Still, he might be useful when it comes to undoing some of what Wilson Hammond is trying to achieve. Even if it turns out that we can't trust him, we might still be able to get some information from him on exactly what they were doing at that lab where we found him.

"You must have guessed something," Jack says to Sebastian. He seems almost as suspicious of his father as I am of Dr. Florence. But then, they've always had a strange relationship. One where they both clearly care about one another, but the needs of the mission come first. "You were preparing for years. These Locations didn't come from nowhere, and the way they're heat shielded…"

118

"You know that we've been monitoring things for decades," Sebastian says. He doesn't sound too upset to be questioned like that. Maybe he's expecting it. "Space, signals, anything we could find that would give us a better grasp on some of the stranger things around us. It doesn't mean that we got things right. Remember that there was a time when we thought Celes here came from space."

Rather than the far future. Because frankly, which of those was more plausible? Well, neither of them, really.

"We thought that because the signals we found coming from Celes seemed to have a celestial connection," Sebastian goes on. I can almost hear the excitement of a scientist there. Sebastian's father has shown that he's interested in helping people first, but finding out new things is definitely a close second for him, even when it makes things more complicated for us.

"So how did you go from that to a place like this?" I ask.

"The possibility of a fire storm or an asteroid strike was always there. Science suggests that the asteroid strike that destroyed the dinosaurs was not going to be an isolated event, for example. There was always the possibility of more impacts. We wanted to be prepared, and with our monitoring, we started to pick up on the heating up of the Earth. Follow me, all of you."

Sebastian leads the way through the main cave, into a room that looks like it might be living quarters. It looks almost like a whole hotel or apartment complex underground. It's a little warmer in here, though still much cooler than it would be out in the desert sun. There's a large dining area, which we walk through to get to a kind of lobby area, where a television is currently displaying images that look like they're taken from a satellite feed.

"There are still satellites?" I ask. "I thought the apocalypse destroyed them. At least, we seemed to lose all communications."

"And we've been working to get them back," Sebastian explains. "We actually launched our own satellite to do it. It wasn't easy. We didn't have the room for a rocket launch, so we had to work with balloons and then small scale rockets from altitude. It's just one of the things we've done to ensure that this Location continues to remain secure in the coming days."

120

"It sounds like you have everything you need for your own little country," I joke.

Sebastian looks a little more serious.

"You aren't actually *thinking* of being a country?" I ask.

He shakes his head. "No, but nor do we intend to be bound by the dictates of any government run by Wilson Hammond. As Faders, our obligation is to do whatever is best for humanity as a whole, and we have always had the resources to operate beyond the limitations of borders and jurisdictions."

"It sounds like you have everything worked out," Jack says.

"Not everything, but we're doing our best. Someone has to preserve things."

Dr. Florence chooses that moment to speak up. "It's good that you are. With the level of destruction there has been, things could go backwards so quickly if no one works to preserve what humanity has learned. One generation not learning is all it would take for the world to regress to the Stone Age."

Fever (FADE #4)

I think about the society we have in the future, where we've had to work so hard to preserve knowledge and advance it. Those thoughts bring me back to Johnny and Grayson. We're down here for a reason, after all.

"Where's Johnny?" I ask. "And what about Grayson? Is he here?"

I hear a laugh from the other side of the room. I turn, unable to keep the happiness out of my expression as I see Grayson there. He looks perfect, unruffled even by the apocalypse, his muscular good looks and short dark hair going together to create a perfect image of the high school jock. Except that Grayson is so much more than that. He used to be so much more than that to me, before Jack.

Grayson actually catches me off guard, picking me up and twirling me in the air, before doing something even more unexpected. He kisses me. Right in front of Jack.

"I'm so glad you survived," Grayson says. "I thought you might be..."

"I'm fine," I say. "Things got a little complicated, but we made it okay."

"Was Johnny with you?" Jack asks, and there's something stern, almost angry, in his voice. It's easy to see why. Grayson is standing there with his arms around me, having just kissed me. A lot of guys would have punched him for doing something like that.

Apparently though, Jack's memories of the future run to remembering that there, at least, the three of us are all good friends. He moves forward to put an arm around Grayson's shoulders.

"You might have your arms around my girl, but it's good to see you made it, buddy."

Grayson shakes his head. "Your girl? Buddy?"

It occurs to me that Grayson hasn't had all the details that Jack and I know about the future yet. He certainly hasn't remembered them for himself. He might never remember them. After all, he didn't come back because of his ability to resist the effects of the Fading machine on memories. He came back after me and Jack. Right now, he might know that we're from the future thanks to seeing some of my memories playing out on the Faders' screens, and he might know all about the

123

apocalypse thanks to the same incident, but he doesn't have the same details Jack and I have.

"Never mind," Jack says. "I'll explain later."

"Right now," I say, "the main thing is that we find Johnny. Is he here, Grayson?"

Grayson looks a little nervous. That isn't like him. "He's here."

"We need to go to him then," I say. "He's going to be vital in helping us treat people when it comes to these plagues. Without him..."

"Just... don't pin your hopes on him," Grayson says. He shakes his head.

"Why?" I ask. "What happened? Sebastian told me about the helicopter ride, but it can't have been that bad can it? Johnny can heal almost anything if he has the tools. Take me to see him."

Grayson swallows. "I'll take you," he says, reaching out to put a hand in mine almost like we're still boyfriend and girlfriend. I'm not sure how I feel about that. "But you have to promise that you won't freak out at what you see. Things didn't go... entirely according to plan."

124

Kailin Gow

THIRTEEN

Jack

Grayson leads Celes away, leaving me with Dr. Florence and my father. I'd rather go with them, *especially* after what has just happened with Grayson. My father, though, has other ideas. He puts a hand on my shoulder, holding me back.

"Jack, Grayson can show Celes Johnny, but for now, we need to debrief. Not all of our Faders made it here."

I look around. It's obvious that there aren't as many Faders in this Location as there should be. The Australian contingent have already told me how many of their people have died. "How bad is it?" I ask.

My father shakes his head. "As far as I can tell, we lost more than half our Faders, including your uncle."

My uncle. His brother in law. My last tie to my mother. I don't know what to say, because this must be hurting Dad as much as me.

I try for professionalism. "What about Lionel and his team?"

"Lionel is missing." A pause. My father knows how close I was to the Faders' trainer. "Half his team made it here, though."

"Only half?" I say.

Dad nods. "That's the part that worries me. Our best team, and even with them, only half made it here. Things… they got pretty brutal in the last couple of days, with the fire storm and everything that happened afterwards

I look over to where Dr. Florence is standing, watching the big screen intently.

"That's just what Dr. Florence here said," I say.

Dad looks over at him too. "Who is he?"

"One of Wilson Hammond's researchers," I explain. "At least until we got him out of that lab. It looked like Hammond wasn't very happy with him anymore. Florence was working in Hammond's lab, doing experiments on people with brain injuries. Apparently, the fire storm caused a reaction to the drugs they were using. They started to absorb solar energy."

"Interesting," Dad says. I can see him running through the problem. "For years, I've been wondering about your mother, Jack, and when Celes came along, that explained a lot. It still didn't quite explain everything though."

"Except that Celes and Mom got to be the way they were because they were from the future," I point out. "People had simply evolved to that point."

Dad nods. I know this is hard for him. Not just talking about Mom, but being wrong. "It never occurred to me that you could be from another time. I thought your mother and Celes were extraterrestrial. It made sense."

Images of kissing Celes flash through me. The feel of her lips against mine. The way she responds to me. "Trust me, Dad, she's all human."

"I've noticed the connection between you," Dad says. "How close were the two of you before you came back here?"

"Very close," I say. "I was her right hand man, along with Grayson and John."

"It's more than that though, isn't it?"

I pause, and then nod, thinking about all the times Celes and I shared together before we came back here. "Yes, it's more than that."

"What exactly did you do in the future before you came back?" Dad asks. He smiles. "I'd like to know more about what my son gets up to besides Fading."

His son. We don't talk about the complexity of the situation. That I'm his son and not his son, all at once. "It's hard to explain," I say instead. "We're older in the future. We'd been working together a while before we came back. Celes... she was the President. I was her head of security."

"And more than that at the same time," Dad says. "It sounds like a complex arrangement."

"It was," I say with a sigh. "For years, we were in a relationship but she wouldn't take it seriously. She wouldn't even think about marrying me. And Grayson... he was an advisor, and he's had pretty serious feelings about her too."

"You're right," Dad says. "It's complicated. But complicated doesn't mean the same thing as impossible. We should know that if anyone does." He reaches out to put a hand on my shoulder. "Now, I think we need to get our mind back on business. We need to talk to Dr. Florence over there and find out what he knows. Because I'm pretty sure that he has a lot more to tell us than he's volunteered so far."

*****

Celes

Grayson takes me out of the room, heading to see Johnny down a hallway, before taking my arm and pulling me into a smaller side room.

"What..." I begin, but I don't have the time to finish the question because in that moment Grayson silences me with a kiss that makes the one he gave me back in the lounge look tame by comparison. With the passion of his mouth on mine, I can't help responding, my hands running over his chest as Grayson kisses me.

"Celes, I thought you wouldn't make it," Grayson says at last, his arms still around me. "I was so worried. I wanted to go back. I wanted to search for you, but I didn't even know where to begin until they got the satellite back up. When they started to pick up your signal, it was like seeing a ghost. No, not a ghost; an angel. I don't think I've ever seen anything more beautiful than that moment."

I hold onto him just as tightly. "I'm glad you're safe too. I missed you so much. I just couldn't... Jack and I have been hidden away from everyone. I didn't know half of what was happening. There wasn't any news. I started to worry that something had happened to you."

"At least you weren't alone," Grayson says. He kisses me again, softly this time. "I hate admitting it, but I'm glad Jack was with you to keep you safe."

"I can burn people to a crisp," I point out. "I'm pretty sure I was safe."

"Did the fact that I can heal almost anything stop you worrying?" Grayson asks. I shake my head. "Well, there you are then."

I reach up to touch his face. I can remember every inch of his skin from when we used to date. I can remember every kiss we had, and the scent of Grayson so close to me. It's a strong, masculine scent that goes well with the feeling of his arms wrapped around me.

"I know we aren't together," Grayson says. "I know how much you love Jack, but after everything that has happened, I can't just ignore what I feel. When I thought you might be gone… I need you, Celes. I loved you in the future, and I love you now. I've always loved you."

"Grayson…" I don't know what to say next. My body doesn't help me, because it responds to Grayson only too readily, but the same is true of Jack. I'm caught between the two of them, and it seems like even when I want to make a decision, circumstances won't let me.

Grayson touches his fingers lightly to my lips. "You don't have to make any decisions now, Celes."

That's the problem. I thought I'd made a decision. Yet here Grayson is, unpicking it just by being there.

"Just give me a chance to show you that I'm the man for you."

Does he even know the man he is? Does he know that Jack and I were together even before we came back here? "How much do you remember about the future?"

132

"When I look at you, when I touch you, I can remember being in high school with you. I can remember all the time we spent together there."

"But that isn't real," I point out.

Grayson shakes his head. "Don't say that. It was real. The other stuff might have been real too, but so was the time we were together as kids. We lived those years too, Celes. And yes, I get other memories creeping in. I can close my eyes and see another, older, version of you. I see an office, and I'm by your side constantly."

Gray hesitates, and I can see the moment when the truth of it comes to him. "You're the president, and I'm you're advisor, and..."

He pushes me back against the wall of the room, and this kiss has his tongue dancing with mine, his body pressed tightly to me. "We're lovers."

I stare at him, trying to tell if he's serious.

"You don't remember?" Grayson asks, looking surprised.

"I thought *you* were the one who didn't remember." We were lovers? I can remember Jack, and I can remember how Grayson felt about me...

Fever (FADE #4)

"All my memories revolve around you, Celes," Grayson says. "We were together, living together. It was the best time of my life, despite everything that was happening."

"I don't remember it," I say.

"Think back," Grayson insists. "The memories are there. You just have to find them. You and I were together for more than a year before you Faded, going after Jack."

I start to say that I don't remember, but in that moment I do, in a flood of memories that make me gasp. Moments with Grayson come back to me in a great tide of images. Of friendship at first, then more. So much more. I can remember moments between us that make me blush when I think of them now and some of the things we did together.

I can remember how it started. Nights spent talking with Grayson simply because he was my closest friend. Telling him about the loneliness when Jack didn't come back. Then the nights when it just seemed so natural to kiss him. To do so much more than that. Grayson convincing me to move on. Grayson persuading me to stay with him.

134

Here and now, he's still kissing me, his hands moving over my skin. And even while he does it, I find myself thinking of Jack. What does all this mean? Where do these new memories fit in? If I lived with Grayson, and as his lips brush my neck, I can remember living with Grayson, does that mean that I stopped loving Jack? If I did, why did I come back after him? Was it really just about the mission, or could I not manage to stay with Grayson when I knew that Jack was out there somewhere?

I don't know what to think. Jack or Grayson? Grayson or Jack? Those thoughts keep running through my head even as Grayson keeps kissing me. I know that I should stop things soon, before they go further, but I'm so busy trying to work out what's going on. It seems like whatever the time period, whatever the situation, the question is the same.

It's a question I have to answer, but the thing is, I know that there *is* no good answer. There is no answer that won't hurt one of them, and the thought of that is almost physically painful. Yet I know I have to choose, no matter how much it is going to hurt.

FOURTEEN

When Grayson finally pulls away from me, I can barely breathe, the kiss has been that intense. It's like Grayson has put all of himself, body and soul, into this one moment. Even Jack would never let himself go so completely with me. Especially Jack. Maybe that's why Grayson and I are apparently so close in the future? I don't know. It's hard to know anything for sure about the future. Harder still to decide what to do now based on it.

Grayson takes my hand. "We should go see Johnny before I take this any further."

"How is he?" I ask, almost grateful for the distraction.

"He's not in any pain, and he's healing. It looks worse than it is, Celes."

"What does?" I demand. "What happened to him? What aren't you telling me?"

Kailin Gow

"Did they tell you that the helicopter we were on crashed in the fire storms?" Grayson asks.

I swallow. I heard that, but if Grayson is standing here unharmed... no, wait, that isn't a guide to anything. I've seen the way Grayson heals.

"What happened?" I ask.

"Everybody but Johnny on that chopper died, Celes. I was able to save him, but even then, it was a close thing. He has severe burns over half his body and face. I was able to get him here in time for him to be out of danger, and we've been working on skin grafts, but he's still in bad shape."

He leads the way to a room that looks like a typical boy's bedroom, except that the bed is obviously a hospital bed; one that can be raised and lowered with the push of a button. Johnny is on that bed, swathed in bandages from the surgery he's had. I can't even see how bad it might be as I move over to take his hand. His big blue eyes stare up at me though, looking cloudy with whatever they've given him to dull the pain and let his body heal.

"Johnny," I say, as gently as I can. "I'm glad you made it. We'll have you back on your feet in no time."

Fever (FADE #4)

"Celestra." Johnny's voice sounds too old for the body holding it. "Thank God you survived. We wouldn't be able to complete our mission without you."

"Forget the mission for now, Johnny," I say. "Just concentrate on getting better."

Johnny squeezes my hand. "The mission is everything. You need to get back to our time. You need to use the Fading machine and bring a cure for everyone, or their fate will be a lot worse than mine."

"You have to get back too, then," I point out. "You're our greatest doctor, not me."

Johnny shakes his head with a kind of grim solemnity that doesn't fit with a child's body. "My body wouldn't take it. In the state I'm in, the dissolution process would probably destroy me completely."

It's my turn to squeeze Johnny's hand. "We need you, John. Do you think any of us has the knowledge to deal with this without you?"

"You need the cure," Johnny insists. "You can find that without me. I've been thinking about this. I've had... plenty of time to think, laying here. We know that the Fever in our time can be traced back to the apocalypse now. We're here, Celestra. This is the moment. If you can find what causes it, the rest doesn't matter."

"So I just have to find the cause of the Fever?" I ask. "I thought I had to stop the apocalypse?"

"It's too late for that now," Johnny points out, and I wince slightly. "No, don't blame yourself. I'm just saying that you need to focus on the cure, not on things that can't be changed. Finding the cause of the Fever should be easier. After all, what is big enough to cause an epidemic thousands of years in the future?"

"I don't know," I admit. There are other things I know I need to ask him. Right now, looking at him, I can't hold back. Even though I know Johnny is healing, because he can't come back with us, it feels more like he's dying, and I can't leave anything unsaid. "There are creatures out there, Johnny. Things that were huge, and they looked like they were part human, part reptile. It was worse than that though. They had abilities. Abilities that were like *mine*, Johnny. They could burn people."

Johnny reaches out towards a table beside the bed, where there's a pad of paper and a pencil. He's too weak to get it for himself, so Grayson has to pass it to him. He draws for almost a minute before showing me what is obviously the same kind of creature as the one that chased Jack and me.

"Like this?" he asks.

I nod. "How did you know?"

"I had theories," Johnny says, "but back in the future, there wasn't enough evidence. It was almost… inconceivable. But the monster you saw… we had reports of them before the Fever hit our time."

"I didn't see those reports," I say.

"Like I said, there wasn't any proof. They said that these creatures bit people, but I couldn't find the bite marks. I thought it was just made up."

"People would run," Grayson says. "They wouldn't let something like that near enough to bite them."

"They're smaller in the future," Johnny says. "And people don't notice small things. Same thing about the way bubonic plague spread with rats. Maybe they don't even need to bite people. It's just a hypothesis. No, not even that, really. Just a guess."

Grayson looks thoughtful. "So, if we could eliminate these things now…"

140

"In theory, it would stop the Fever in the future," Johnny says. "Easy."

"Except for the part where they're ten feet tall and nearly unstoppable," I say.

"How do they get to be so much smaller in the future?" Grayson asks. "I wouldn't have thought that being smaller would be an evolutionary advantage."

Johnny shrugs. "Lots of animals are smaller than they used to be. Look at the size crocodiles used to be around the time of the dinosaurs. Or most of the huge mammals following that. Sometimes, being smaller means that you don't have to find as much food."

"What about the burning?" I ask.

"Environmental conditions may have triggered that," Johnny says. "It isn't necessarily significant."

"It was the experiments we did, combined with the solar storm."

I turn to see that Dr. Florence has come into the room, along with Sebastian Cook and Jack.

"These creatures were part of your experiments?" I say. "I thought you experimented on people with brain issues?"

Fever (FADE #4)

"We kept reptiles and large insects for experiments which were too dangerous for humans," Dr. Florence explains. "The simpler way their brain works even compared to most mammals means that we were able to explore certain aspects more directly, including looking into some diseases that for obvious reasons we couldn't introduce to human hosts."

"So the Fever could be a mutation of one of those diseases?" Grayson asks. "And the creatures we saw…"

"They could be a combination of the creatures we used for our experiments and some of the humans we brought in for them," Dr. Florence admits. "I'm sorry. We really were trying to help people."

"How?" I ask. "What exactly were you trying to do to those people?"

"They had memory lapses," Dr. Florence explains. "Blackouts. Lost time. Most of them, when they became emotional, wouldn't have the rational control over it that you or I would have. They would simply act on whatever they felt immediately. It could make them violent, in many cases. Even in the mildest cases, they have limited attention spans."

142

"My parents thought that I had ADD when I was young," I say, remembering. "I couldn't concentrate well then. That just made me frustrated. Angry. It was only when I started running… running helped me to deal with it."

"You aren't the same as them," Jack says, moving closer to me.

"Aren't I?" I look to Dr. Florence. "Aren't I the kind of person you would have experimented on?"

"The kind of person we would have tried to help, Celes," Dr. Florence says. "And yes, you would have fallen at the milder end of that spectrum, only it sounds like you found an outlet that allowed you to deal with those problems in a more constructive manner."

"You're Dr. Florence. The scientist involved in my fa… Senator Hammond's experiments on people?"

"What do you know about that?" Dr. Florence asks. He sounds worried.

"My father wanted me to go there," Johnny says. "He wanted to alter my memories and strange behavior, until he found out about the Fading technology. He thought you might be able to cure me of this."

"That might have been how he started," Dr. Florence says, "but it didn't finish up like that. By the end, he wanted me to kill everyone there."

Johnny looks shocked by that. I reach down to squeeze his hand.

"It's okay, Johnny. I know that Wilson Hammond is one of our targets, but he's also your father in this time. The trouble is, he isn't what you want him to be. He was the one who was able to bring down the fire storm to start the apocalypse. He's the one who brought all this down on us. I think, if there was ever anything good in him, it's gone now."

"I..." Johnny's look of shock turns to one of horror, and I wish I could hug him, but with the burns, it simply wouldn't be safe.

"Johnny, you deserve to know this," I say. "Hammond isn't a good man. Be ready to run and fight if he comes for you. He's not the man you grew up with, and he isn't interested in your well-being anymore. He's the beast. The one who brings the apocalypse. We can't trust him, and we have to try to stop what he's doing. You understand that, don't you?"

144

Johnny looks down and sighs. "I'm not a kid, Celes. Well, no, that's the problem. I am a kid. I'm a kid and one of our time's leading scientific minds at the same time, and it's enough to tear me apart. You think this is bad for you, Jack, and Grayson? At least you're yourselves. There are only a few years in it. I… my mind tells me exactly how dangerous Wilson Hammond is, but at the same time, everything in my experience in this body tells me something different. It wants to believe that he's better than that."

"He isn't. Remember who you really are, Johnny."

Johnny looks up at me. "Who are we really, Celes? Are these bodies just covers we can cast aside? They're real, produced by the machines, but real. We grew to this age the same way kids did, and now we're expected to put all that aside. How easy are you finding that, Celes?"

I think about Jack and Grayson then. Grayson, for whom I feel so much, not because I can remember our time together in the future, but because I can remember running with him in high school. Because I can remember him as my first kiss, even though he *wasn't*. Not really.

Fever (FADE #4)

"We can't let this be personal," I say, though I've already done that. I allowed the apocalypse, after all. "We have to do the job and go home."

FIFTEEN

Seeing Johnny like this, hearing him talk about the Fever, I can feel more memories stirring up in my mind. I dive down into them, hoping that they might have answers. I can see myself consulting with a team of scientists, sitting around a table and looking grave.

"It looks like the southeastern corner of the US was first," one says, reading from a file, and I can hear myself sigh.

"Then the East Coast, the West Coast, the middle, everywhere else… it doesn't help us if we don't know how it's spreading."

The memory fades, and I'm left looking at Dr. Florence, who is sitting in a corner now while doctors fuss around Johnny.

"Dr. Florence. What's the connection between these creatures and people who can manipulate energy?"

147

He knows. I'm sure he knows. It's just a question of finally getting some answers from him.

"I can tell you more about the condition, but I'm not so sure about the creatures. We know that all those suffering from the impairments we were working on had a very similar biological and neurological makeup. In particular, they tended to have very overactive brain waves. That activity has to be fueled by something."

"By what?" I ask.

"In an immediate way, by the food they eat, the same way all humans are. Yet how does food work? Ultimately, it is a chain leading back to the sun. Plats photosynthesize energy and store it within themselves. Animals eat the plants. Omnivores like humans eat both. At each stage, it is about precious energy from the sun, locked up in different forms."

"I don't see how that helps us to understand what's going on," I point out.

"The solar storm clearly altered their brainwaves to allow them to access that more directly," Dr. Florence explains.

"So I don't need to eat?"

"I'm not sure it works as simply as that."

"Well, how does it make for a connection between the two?" I ask.

Dr. Florence shrugs. "Well, I suppose the same thing must have happened with the creatures, so possibly, theoretically at least, understanding the brains of those with this condition might allow them to understand the creatures better. As a purely theoretical exercise."

"No." I shake my head and try to remember how I sound in the future. Authoritative. Presidential. "This is *not* a theoretical exercise. We face a mass epidemic in the future, which we call the Fever. Johnny is telling me that these creatures are behind it, and if we don't get it under control, then the whole of humanity could be wiped out. Does that sound like a theoretical problem to you, Dr. Florence?"

"I don't understand what you want me to do," the scientist says.

I try to explain. "Our best hope of ridding the world of the Fever in the future is to destroy those creatures now, before they have a chance to spread it. Only they aren't small pests now. We can't exactly just step on them and squash them. I've been chased by one of these things. They're fast, they're powerful, and their skin is tough enough to deflect low caliber bullets. Plus they can burn people. We'd need an army to stop them through straight ahead force."

"I still don't understand what you want from me," Dr. Florence says.

I grab him, lifting him out of his seat. It's a bullying move, but right now, I get the impression that Dr. Florence does his best work when he's scared. "I need you to find us a weakness in them. Find us a way to strip away their powers, so that we might actually have a chance to end this. Don't tell me that you can't do it. After all, you did more than enough research on them for Hammond."

Dr. Florence obviously understands the threat there. We haven't forgotten what he did for Hammond. "I guess... we *could* try to reverse the effects of the solar storm. If we could reverse that, then in theory, we might be able to undo the effects. After all, if that had never happened, then none of what followed would have been a problem."

It seems that I'm not the only one capable of reminding people about the past. Guilt weighs down on me again as I think about Wilson Hammond. I let him live. I wouldn't let Jack kill him, because I thought he could still be saved, and that decision cost millions of people their lives. No matter what Dr. Florence has done in the past, what I've done is worse.

"I wish I had a better answer for you," Dr. Florence says. "Then we wouldn't have these... *things* running around killing people. Disintegrating them."

"I have that ability," I say. "If you work on me, would anything you came up with apply to them?"

"It... might," Dr. Florence admits.

"So, if you were to try to reverse my powers, we could come up with a way to weaken these creatures?"

Dr. Florence looks at me seriously then. "Do you really want to give up such important gifts? They help to make you who you are."

I shake my head. "No, they don't. They don't define me, and they never have. For years, I was just a girl who liked to run. I didn't know anything about being able to

151

burn people to death, and I *certainly* don't want that to be the main thing that defines me."

"But you're willing to risk giving it up."

"To save the world?" I almost laugh. "Dr. Florence, there have been days when I wished I never had these abilities. Giving them up to protect people is a *tiny* price to have to pay."

Dr. Florence takes my hand. "If you really want to do this, then we'll have to get you into the lab and sedate you. Some of the procedures I need to do will be quite... invasive."

"Wait, Celes." Jack is there beside me then. "You're really going to let Dr. Florence experiment on you, just like that?"

"It's for a good cause, Jack. If he can remove my ability, then he could remove it from these creatures, too."

"Possibly," Jack says. "Assuming that you trust him enough to do it."

"There would be other scientists around. Even your dad."

Jack half turns me away from Dr. Florence. "Is this about helping people, or just getting rid of your ability?"

"We could find a way to help other people with this problem, Jack," I say.

"It isn't a problem," Jack insists. "It's a gift. One that makes you very special."

"Special enough to kill people," I say, remembering the people I've killed. Most of them didn't even have enough time to scream while they burned, but a few did, and in my memories, those are the ones who come back to me. "Special enough to burn them alive until there's nothing left. Special enough to *want* to do that. You've seen what I'm like when I get angry, Jack. It's a curse. A curse that does nothing but kill people."

"It could if it isn't used properly," Jack says, "but you've used it to save lives. Tell her, Grayson."

"Most of us wouldn't be here if it weren't for you, Celes," Grayson says. "The only people you've killed have been ones who were trying to kill you, and I would have killed them if you hadn't."

He says that now, but I can remember the horror in his eyes while I've burned people.

"Are you sure you want to do this, Celes?" Jack asks. "Your powers have let you help a lot of people. They let you burn us a way out of the Others' base. They let us save your parents. They even let us start the car on the way here. We wouldn't have escaped that creature without you. Are you sure you want to give that up?"

I know that Jack is making sensible points, but I nod my head anyway. "If it means that I can cut off the source of the problem now, then yes. I'd give up my abilities in a heartbeat. I let Hammond live, Jack. You could have stopped the apocalypse, and I let it happen. If this is what it takes to fix things, then I have to do it. If *dying* is what it takes to fix things, then that's what I'll do."

"Don't talk like that, Celes," Grayson says. "We aren't going to let you die here."

"But you aren't going to stop me from doing this, either," I say. My mind is made up. I have to let Dr. Florence try.

"You understand that we might not succeed straight away?" the scientist says. "It could be a long, and potentially dangerous, process."

"I understand," I say. When has any part of this ever been safe? "Let's just get on with it."

154

"Okay." Dr. Florence reaches out for my hand again, but in that moment, there's a lot of excited talking outside the door. It opens to reveal Niall, the leader of the Australian Faders.

"Dr. Cook, Jack, you're going to want to see this."

"Can't it wait, Niall?" Jack asks.

"Not unless you want to miss out on a bonza opportunity. While you've been down here, we got a call about a team out in the desert, and we went out to help them. I mean, Outback is Outback, right? Me and the boys went out to help, and we got to them okay, but then we came across this... creature. Looked just like the one you were talking about before, Jack. Part reptile, part insect, part human. It almost burned Vincent, even after we put a few rounds into it. Thought it was going to take us all arvo to bring it down."

"You killed it?" I ask. If they've managed to kill one of the creatures, that's a good thing, but it doesn't change anything.

"We didn't kill it," Niall explains. "We managed to subdue it. And *you* try finding things to tie up a creature

155

that can burn through almost anything. Not to mention bringing it back on the jeep."

"You've brought it here?" I say.

"Well, we weren't going to leave it out in the desert, were we?" Niall says.

We follow him, leaving Johnny behind in the care of the doctors. Niall leads the way along a series of corridors, past a door that's sealed with heavy locks. Behind it, there's a cage, though it seems to be made out of the non-burning material the Faders use rather than steel.

Inside, there's one of the creatures. It seems almost too big for the cage, it's strange, part insect, part reptile body filling the space almost completely.

"Of course," Niall says, "it isn't exactly much to look at, but I thought you might want it anyway."

I look around at the others. Dr. Florence, Sebastian, and Jack all seem to be thinking the same thing. Jack nods to the creature.

"If Celes could maybe tell us something about stopping those things, one of *them* will tell us so much more. We need to find a way to sedate it and then get it into the lab."

SIXTEEN

We head across to another lab, where it takes Dr. Florence almost a half hour to get set up. In that time, I see medical personnel wheeling Johnny across in his hospital bed.

"You didn't think I'd miss out on the opportunity to do this, did you?" Johnny asks.

"You should be resting," I insist. "We can do this without you."

"Well, that's *one* way to make me feel useless," Johnny says. "Celes, I want to help. I *should* help. If anyone can help to find a way to deal with this problem, it's me."

I realize that despite arguing, he's still asking me for permission. Whatever else is happening, I'm still his president.

"Okay, Johnny, but if it gets too much, we'll get you out of here, okay?"

"Okay."

158

The creature that the Australian Faders have captured is out of its cage now. It's a risk, but the scientists need to get to it if they're going to work on it. It's sedated, suspended within a network of wires coated with heat resistant materials. It looks strange. An impossible blend of creatures that is somehow bigger than all of them. Dr. Florence, Sebastian, a couple of the Australian Faders and a few more scientists stand around it, working with a wide variety of machinery.

"What are you going to do?" I ask Dr. Florence.

"We're going to start by getting as much information as possible," he says. "Physiological, neurological... as much data as we can find. That will make it easier to understand if these creatures have any obvious weaknesses that can be exploited."

"Do you think they will have any?" I ask.

Jack answers, moving to stand next to me. "Everything has a weakness, Celes."

I wonder what mine is. Is it him? Grayson? The way my heart seems to jump between them almost at random, leaving me breathless and unable to make up my mind what I want? Unable even to think when they're close.

159

That has to be a weakness, doesn't it? Yet it's not one I think I'm going to be able to do anything about.

"What are you going to do first?" I ask Dr. Florence, trying not to think about Jack or Grayson too much. Here, in a confined space with both of them, it's impossible.

"We're going to check its brainwaves first," Dr. Florence explains. "I want to be in a position to see how they respond to different stimuli."

"We can't do too much on that front," Sebastian points out. "After all, the creature isn't conscious, and we are *not* about to wake it up to check. In fact, we should work faster. We have no way of knowing how its hybrid physiology will process the sedative."

"It's one of the questions I'm hoping to answer in the course of this investigation," Dr. Florence says.

"Well, let's not do it by being burned to death."

Technicians hurry around them, attaching pads to the creature's skull, linked by wires to computer screens that start to show data. Dr. Florence starts to press buttons and the data changes. It's hard to feel useful in that moment, standing there watching other people work.

160

I'm meant to be at the heart of this mission, but right now, I just don't have the scientific skills to make a contribution.

"There are brain waves going all over the place," Dr. Florence says. "And a complex brain. More complex than insect ones, or even reptiles, yet different to mammalian ones as well. It's like the structures of the brain are designed specifically for the manipulation of energy."

"Is it the same with mine?" I ask.

"Close, maybe," Johnny answers from his bed, "but not the same. These things' brains aren't human."

Dr. Florence starts to push more buttons.

"What are you checking now?" Grayson asks, from the side of the room.

"I want to examine the creature's metabolic rate. If what we know about their speed and strength is true, then a high metabolic rate might fit in with that. It also makes sense in terms of their ability to manipulate energy."

The numbers on the screen spike as Dr. Florence makes a few more adjustments. "Incredible. Everything about these creatures is fast. What interests me, if they use such vast amounts of energy, is how that energy is transported around the body."

"What do you mean?" I ask.

"Well, in humans, we get energy through a variety of physical systems, but the most important one is the heart carrying oxygenated blood around the body. With the size of these creatures, their cardio-vascular systems must have enlarged considerably, but I think it might be even more complicated than that."

"Why?" I ask. Eventually, Dr. Florence is going to give us an answer that we can use.

"Because insects don't really have hearts as we know them, or even the same kind of blood," Dr. Florence explains. "Instead, they have an integrated circulatory system where hemolymph, the closest thing they have to blood, flows through the whole body. They have a kind of dorsal vessel that does a similar job to the heart in pumping it around, but it isn't the same."

"So what are you expecting to see?" Jack asks. "An enlarged dorsal vessel? A combination of it with a heart?"

"Something like that, possibly," Dr. Florence says. "We won't know until we've done an ultrasound or MRI of its main body cavity."

They opt for the MRI when Sebastian's technicians come forward with equipment that lets them do it far more portably than would normally be possible. Yet another piece of technology the Faders have that the rest of the world does not. The results take just a minute or two to come up on the screen.

"No," Johnny says, staring at it, "that can't be right."

"What can't be?" I ask, not sure what it is that I'm meant to be seeing. I need to understand, and not just because it might give us a way to deal with these creatures. It might also tell me more about the way my body works.

"I'm no expert on insectoid physiology," Johnny says, "but that looks like they have acquired a heart in addition to the usual dorsal vessel."

"That's what I'm seeing," Sebastian confirms, moving to stand beside Dr. Florence.

"So what's the problem?" I ask.

163

Fever (FADE #4)

Dr. Florence shakes his head, taking a step back from the equipment. He looks over at the creature, lit by the bright lighting of the room, as though he might be able to figure out what is going on just by looking at it.

"The problem," he explains, "is that neither one is really sufficient to supply the energy needs of a creature this size. Perhaps if both systems are working together?"

"But then they'd be in conflict," Sebastian points out. "The body doesn't have two systems to do one job, because they'd get in each other's way. They'd balance for a time, but if they got out of balance..."

I look around their faces. "How did this happen?"

"It must be a side effect of the solar storm," Sebastian says. "The transformation enlarged them and started to change their physiology, but the process isn't complete."

"That would explain why they go back to being small," I say. "They aren't stable at this size."

"But they still take back enough changes to bring about the Fever," Jack points out.

I nod. "Could this mix of hearts be our way to stop them? It sounds like if they were put under any kind of stress, they could have a heart attack really easily."

"In theory, that could work," Sebastian admits. "But actually doing it would be harder. We've already seen that fighting or chasing prey won't do it, so what would?"

"We'll think of something," Grayson says. "For now, the important thing is that we know of a way to destroy them without risking the lives of the few people that we have."

"We can experiment on this one," Dr. Florence suggests. "If we try out a range of stimuli, we can find one that will stress the creature enough to make its new circulatory system fail."

I notice that he doesn't seem to have any qualms about conducting potentially fatal experiments on the creatures. Is that just that they aren't human, or is Dr. Florence maybe not the humanitarian that he wants us to think he is? After all, we only have his word for it that he left Hammond because he didn't like experimenting on humans.

That's a matter for another time now, though. The fact is that we know enough about these creatures to potentially destroy them. If we can do that...

I turn to Jack. "We could stop the Fever. We could do what we came here to do. If we manage it, we might even be able to go home. I mean, we have the Fading machines."

"We'd *have* to go home," Jack says. "We'd have to check that the future changes the way it is meant to change."

Even Grayson seems to agree with that. "If we don't, then we could find that the Fever still finds a way to come through that we don't know about. We need to eradicate these things, then get back to our time."

I nod, though the truth is that we're getting a long way ahead of ourselves. First, we still have to destroy the creatures, and even with what we know, that won't be easy. After all, we still haven't thought of anything that will be enough to terrify a huge, part reptile, part insect creature to death.

I try to focus on smaller things. "Dr. Cook," I say to Sebastian, "can you get what we've learned to other

166

Faders? I assume that there must still be some out in other areas of the world. Plus, there will be the populations who made it to the shelters. If they at least know about this weakness, then maybe they can find ways to exploit it so that they aren't all killed by the creatures."

"We have satellite communications again, as well as more advanced signaling equipment. If there's anybody listening, then we should be able to reach them without a problem."

An idea comes to me. I don't know if it will work or not, but it has to be worth a try.

"Can we use the satellite to create more visual effects too?" I ask.

"It's not what it was designed for, but I guess if we reprogram some of the onboard circuitry, we could probably do it." Sebastian looks at me. "What are you thinking, Celes?"

I'm thinking that there's one thing in the world that is guaranteed to scare every living thing on it. One thing that these creatures definitely know about, and which even they must surely be terrified of.

Fever (FADE #4)

"It's very simple," I explain. "We're going to do the one thing that might scare even these things enough to get their hearts beating. We're going to re-create the apocalypse."

SEVENTEEN

In a control room deeper in the rock spur, Sebastian stands in front of the controls for the Faders' satellite. I've been watching him and some of the other scientists there working for hours now, as they try to make the necessary modifications for this plan. Some of them have seemed a little reluctant, saying that it might damage parts of the satellite that sound important, but Sebastian has been able to keep them working. He's still their boss, apocalypse or no apocalypse.

"*Will* it destroy the satellite?" I ask.

Sebastian shrugs. "It probably won't go that far, but we're using it for a purpose for which it was never intended, effectively using it as a giant projector, with the clouds as our screen, while simultaneously sending out signals to every functioning TV and radio that we can find. It probably won't last for more than a day or so before burning out."

"I'm sorry," I say. "It seems like you've had nothing but trouble since I showed up."

Sebastian shakes his head. "It's what we're here for, Celes. This moment is what the Faders are about. And this is for my son, too."

"Even though Jack isn't your son?"

"He is in every sense that matters. Mechanical things can be fixed. I can put a new satellite up. We've even rebuilt the Fading machine. People matter more."

With that, he flips a switch on the control panel and stands back.

"There," he says, "it's done. I just hope you know what you're doing, Celes."

"So do I," I admit.

We go to watch the screens in the main common room. They're picking up fragments of news feeds as well as data from Faders around the world. Most importantly, there's a feed from the cameras Location Thirteen has pointed at the outside.

Those cameras let us see it as it starts, the sky seeming to turn red all at once, flames appearing to dance across it. I know it's just the cloud formations above us

170

shifting, but even so, my heart is in my mouth. It looks so much like what happened before. Then I see the flames seeming to pour down from the sky.

On the news feeds, there are pictures of people screaming and running, in those cities that still have a meaningful population left. There are a few images of the creatures that have been burning people, and those look almost as frightened as the people. More frightened, because suddenly, some of them are being targeted with flames.

"Faders with flame throwers," Jack explains, as on the screen the strange, hybrid creatures start to run about in utter terror. "I thought it would be a nice touch."

Nice is probably the wrong word for it, but it works. I see the first creatures fall as they run, bellowing inhumanly and then collapsing to the ground as their hearts give way. There are so many people running by that point that they just trample the creatures, mashing them down into the dirt beneath their soles.

"It's working," I say. "It's *working*."

Slowly, though. The satellite can only be over so much of the world at a time. Its coverage is limited, and to stop the Fever, we need to eliminate *all* the creatures. We can't risk leaving some of them behind. I think we all know that, because all of us who aren't doing anything: me, Jack, Grayson, Johnny and more, find ourselves stuck in front of those screens, watching what the few news services still running are calling the Obliteration. They're right, but it's the Obliteration of the creatures, not of humanity. It might just *save* humanity.

That's when I glance back to the screen for the outside cameras, and I see what's coming.

"Jack, Grayson, Sebastian! We're under attack!"

There are helicopters on the screen. One is a very familiar shape that chased us down from the research facility. Others seem to be transport helicopters. It seems like Hammond didn't lose us after all. He was just going to get reinforcements.

"Everybody to their stations," Sebastian orders. "We have to defend the base. There is nowhere else to go."

Faders hurry to grab guns and flak jackets as outside, heavily armed men start to rappel down from their helicopters. Hammond's attack chopper fires missiles and I can feel Location Thirteen shaking.

Faders rush to guard the entrances, and outside the room I can hear the chatter of gunfire. A couple of soldiers burst in carrying automatic weaponry. Jack and Grayson bring up their own guns at almost the same moment to drop them, before moving forward to grab their rifles. Shots rip through Grayson in that moment, and Jack drags him back while I gasp at the thought of him being hurt like that.

Then he stands up, and I remember again why he's the one person I *don't* need to worry about.

"The satellite is locked," Sebastian says, working the controls. "They can't change it now."

"You're saying that like we can't hold them here," Dr. Florence says. He looks as scared as ever. "If Mr. Hammond takes us…"

"We're losing people," Sebastian snaps back at him. "This is not the time for you to be a coward."

There's a burst of gunfire from outside the room followed by silence.

"We need to fall back," Jack says. "Everybody out."

173

"Where are we heading though?" I ask. "If Hammond is inside, where is there that's safe?"

Jack looks at Sebastian. "You said that you'd rebuilt the Fading machine?"

Sebastian hesitates, and then nods. "It's ready. It will work."

"Our mission's done, Celes," Jack says. "The creatures are gone. There won't be a Fever. We need to go back."

"What about Hammond?" I demand. "What about all the people here?"

"You're our priority here, Celes," Grayson insists, taking over from Jack. "You and the machine."

"They'll destroy it if they can," Johnny says, standing awkwardly.

I try to answer that, but Grayson and Jack nod to one another. They grab one of my arms each, turning back to fire bursts of automatic fire as Hammond's men try to come into the room. I see one of the Australians, Ray I think, go down.

"We need to go *now,* Celes," Jack insists, and now I'm ready to listen.

We run, all of us. Jack and Grayson keep me ahead of them, leapfrogging one another as they fire back at the soldiers who pop out behind us around corners. Sebastian and Dr. Florence help Johnny. There's no sign of any of the Australians. They're gone. Probably dead. There's something tragic about that thought; that they could have come thousands of miles through the apocalypse just to be shot in a corridor somewhere. But I know that they're all Faders, and it's what they have signed up for. The way I signed up for a mission that might soon be over.

Between us, we keep moving in the direction of the room they've rebuilt the Fading machine in. When we get there, Sebastian throws the doors open, letting us all pile inside, then locks them behind us. Jack and Grayson wedge a bench behind them.

"That won't hold them for long," Jack says. "We need to go."

The Fading machine is everything I remember it being. A large chair with a much larger device looming over it, straps on the chair bringing back memories of the time they tried to Fade my identity. There's no time to

175

think about that though, because already there are thuds as booted feet slam into the door.

"We need to hurry," Jack says. "If they destroy the machine again, we might never get back home. Grayson, go first and make sure it's safe."

Grayson lets Jack strap him in. I move over to Grayson while Jack works on the control panel. I kiss him, because I can't *not* kiss him at a moment like this, when he's about to be disintegrated, effectively killed in this time so that he can be remade in the future.

"It's fine, Celes," Grayson says. "I'll see you there."

The machine hums as power draws up through it, then whines as its energy flashes through Grayson. Blue light seems to run through Grayson, and then he's gone. Just… gone.

"Johnny," Jack says, "you're next. We'll have to risk it and hope that you're strong enough to survive."

Johnny nods and Jack straps him in. Jack sets the controls again. There's a crack from the doors and they burst open, revealing Wilson Hammond. His normally handsome older features are twisted by anger, and his expensive suit is torn.

176

"No! You will not take my son!"

He lunges for the machine. For Johnny. It's too late. The machine flashes, and Johnny is gone too.

"No," Hammond says, and in that moment there's the glow around him that there was before the apocalypse. The shape of another, larger creature shifting around his. "You cannot have Johnny. His destiny lies here, as my son. He is the one who will help me create a new world. One with beings in it suited to rule it. One that is strong, not weak, like the one you create."

He stares at me while he says that.

"He's gone, Hammond," I say. "You can't get him back."

"Then you won't be *going* back," Hammond replies, and lunges for the machine. Jack intercepts him with a punch, but Hammond spins and smashes him aside. Jack bounds back, tackling Hammond low and bearing them both to the floor.

"Celes," he yells, "get in. Dad, set the machine!"

I don't want to leave him, but Sebastian pushes me back into the chair, setting the straps so tight that I can't break free without destroying the Fading machine. I see

Jack flipping past Hammond's legs, moving to pin him down while throwing punches. Hammond grabs him and throws him off, but Jack charges in again to control him. I realize that's all he's trying to do. Just slow Hammond down long enough to let me get away.

Sebastian is working the controls by now, setting them again the way he did for Johnny, his face an intense mask of concentration. Jack, meanwhile, is barely managing to hold Hammond. It shouldn't work like that. He's younger and fitter, not to mention a skilled fighter. Yet with the strength of the Beast in him, Hammond is so much harder to stop.

"Hurry!" Jack yells over.

"Jack!"

"Celes, I love you! Go!"

Unlike Grayson, I don't even get to kiss Jack goodbye. He's too busy fighting with Hammond. He's done this so many times now, staying behind to keep me alive. I told him not to do this. I *told* him not to. Yet ultimately, I'm not sure anything could stop him. Jack is Jack, and he'll always do whatever he needs to do to protect me, whatever time period it is.

Kailin Gow

I just hope, as I hear the whine of the Fading machine, that he'll be able to do it in the future too. I strain against the straps, wanting to help him, but Sebastian throws the switch in that moment. The light is blinding, and there's a moment of agony as every cell of my body rips apart. Then there's nothing.

EIGHTEEN

I blink and slowly, the world comes back into focus. I can see people standing around me, and the first of them I see is Grayson. He's the way he was. Still a teenager, not a man. How did that happen? The Fading machine, I realize. When it sent us back, it sent us back as babies, because it didn't have the ability to add in the effects of aging. Now that it has returned us... well, no one has ever returned. How were we to know what the effects would be?

There's another figure beside him. John. John's leaning against the wall breathlessly, but that isn't the strangest part. He isn't a boy anymore. Not a boy, but not a grown man either. An acne featured teenager with oily hair stands in front of me, skinny, almost malnourished looking.

"John, Grayson? Are we back?"

180

Grayson smiles widely, heading over to a cabinet, which he opens, revealing equipment that we all stowed before heading back.

"It seems everything is where it should be. Welcome back, Madam President."

Back. We're back. What does that mean? What has happened while we've been away? How long have we even been away? The Fading machine could have returned us a second after we left, or twenty years. We won't know until we look. Talking of looking...

"How old am I?" I ask.

Grayson steps forward, touching my face. "You're you. You're exactly as you were. Apparently the machine doesn't do as much to change people's ages coming this way."

"John's different, though. How are you, John?"

John looks down at the body he has now. "It's not too bad. Given the shape I was in when I left, I'm lucky that the machine was able to bring me back together at all. There are worse fates than being a teenager."

Fever (FADE #4)

Grayson's hands go to my shoulders, rubbing away knots of tension I didn't know I had. "How are you?" he asks. "Disoriented? Okay?"

"I'm fine," I assure him, though honestly I don't know whether I am or not. How much can I remember? "Jack..."

John looks concerned, staring at the Fading machine as Grayson helps me out of it. "Where is Jack? Was he right behind you?"

"I don't know," I admit. "He was fighting Hammond, trying to buy me time. I don't know if he succeeded, or if he'll even be coming back."

That thought makes me choke back a sob, and despite all the rivalry Grayson must feel for Jack, he holds me close.

"It's going to be okay," Grayson promises. "Jack has pulled through impossible situations before. If anyone can get back here, it's him."

There's the whine of the Fading machine behind me then, and I turn, hope lighting up in my heart in that moment as a male body starts to be constructed on it. It's like watching a sculptor work, the body coming through

182

roughly in the first few seconds, then in more and more detail.

"Jack?" I start forward. Grayson tries to stop me, but he's too slow. He's not going to keep me back from Jack. I want to be there when he opens his…

It isn't Jack. As the machine fills in the last details, it's obvious who it is. Wilson Hammond. A little younger maybe, but still definitely him as his eyes snap open and he looks up at me with obvious hatred. I start to pull back, but he's at least as fast as I am. He surges to his feet, grabbing my arm and twisting it behind my back almost to the point of breaking it. I cry out in pain as he does it, and Hammond makes a sound almost of pleasure at that. He's enjoying me being hurt.

"Let her go!" Grayson orders.

"No," Hammond says. "I don't think so. Celes here is coming back with me, so that we can make everything the way it needs to be. She can do that. She's *good* at that. I certainly can't allow her to be here."

"Let her go," John says, and for a moment he sounds like little Johnny again. "Dad, you've already caused the world enough suffering."

Fever (FADE #4)

I can't see Hammond looking across to John, but I can hear his small sound of disappointment. "And you're here too, Johnny. You could have done so much with me back there, you know. You could have helped me come up with diseases even more beautiful than the Fever. You are, after all, brilliant."

"You're mad," John says. "Haven't you hurt people enough?"

"No," Hammond replies. "Not nearly enough. You see, thanks to Celes here, humanity survived the first apocalypse, *and* the second. My Fever. My beautiful Fever. It took such a lot of work to design, and she undid that work in less than a day."

"You need to let her go," John insists. "It's over. You have no issues with Celes."

"Aside from her ruining my plan?" Hammond asks. "She can't be president here anymore. If she is, well, humanity might just keep on surviving, and I am *sick* of humanity. So very sick of it."

"We've stopped the Fever?" Even with Hammond holding me so painfully, that's good to hear. The idea that my people might be safe is the best news I've heard, not just for a while, but in either of the lives I've lived. "Wait, how do you know that? You just arrived. And what you're saying..."

"I know a lot," Hammond replies, and his voice is like oil pouring over me. "I know things that humans cannot comprehend. You know who I am, Celestra. I've told you before. I've *shown* you before."

As he says that, I can feel it. The evil rising up from him; pouring off him in waves. It is like the foul stench of rotting meat, but it isn't just a scent. This runs soul deep. The hairs on my arms are standing on end just being this close to him.

I thought I knew about the evil in Hammond. I thought I'd seen it in the apocalypse. I thought that he was the Antichrist, but standing here, I'm starting to think that even that might not be enough to describe him. I thought he was a man who had been taken by something else, but I was wrong. Very, very wrong.

Hammond spins me to face him, and his face glows almost beautifully, while at the same time looking at him is the most terrifying experience of my life. He holds me by the hair, making me look into eyes that saw the birth of the world.

"Do you know who I am yet?" he asks. "Do you know *what* I am?"

I know.

"The Devil. You're the Devil."

Heat rises from Hammond then. The heat of the sun? The heat of Hell? No wonder he was able to call down fire storms. The thought of everything he's done so far makes me shiver, despite the heat running over me.

"I am indeed, human girl." Hammond's smile is like diamonds. Cold and unyielding. "I am he whom God tried to make bow down to his newest creations, and who was cast down because he would not. Do you know how long I have worked to destroy you, never working directly? Never working in my full form? Do you know how long I had to think and plan before I came up with the idea of coming down as one of you? Though obviously, I stole that one from Him."

I stare at Hammond with increasing horror. I thought before that there might be some way to reason with him. I thought afterwards that we'd managed to stop his plans, and that he couldn't affect us in the future, but this…

"Beautiful, wasn't it?" Hammond asks. "Working as a human, in human ways, without even resorting to my supernatural form."

"Because you aren't allowed to. Not without permission."

At the sound of Jack's voice, I try to turn, and Hammond pulls me back against him tightly. Jack is there, jumping off the Fading machine.

"Jack!" I yell. "You made it!"

I surge towards him again, but Hammond pulls me back. "I'm going to enjoy tormenting you when this is done," he says. "But first, you are going to come back and help me end this."

I try to ignore him, speaking to Jack instead. "How did you get back?"

"It wasn't easy," Jack says. "Hammond had a lot of men with him."

"Yes," Hammond says, "I did."

Fever (FADE #4)

"And there were a lot of casualties," Jack adds, ignoring Hammond. He obviously understands what I'm trying to do.

"Yes," Hammond says. "How did that feel, Jack?"

Jack keeps ignoring him. "Including Dr. Florence and my father."

I swallow. That's hard to bear. I can only imagine how much it must hurt Jack right now to know that Sebastian Cook, the man who brought him up, is gone.

"That's hard, Jack," I say. "I'm so sorry. I only wish..."

"Stop ignoring me!" Hammond yells, almost exactly like a petulant child, and that's the moment when I stamp down with all the power I can muster on his foot. I think I can hear bone breaking. I can certainly feel his grip loosen. I snap my head back, slamming it into his and ignoring the pain that comes from it. I drop, letting my weight go limp, then drive forward away from Hammond as I slip from his now barely there grip. I imagine that I can feel his hands snatching for the space where I was standing just a moment before as I throw myself forward way from him.

188

John and Grayson catch me and I spin around, facing Hammond.

"You think that's enough?" Hammond demands. "I am *taking* you back, Celes. I am taking you back, and you are going to help me destroy this mistake of a future."

I shake my head. "Never."

"I wasn't planning on giving you a choice. Though if you don't want to do it, perhaps you'd like to see me in my real form? Perhaps you'd like me to destroy this place *that* way?"

I swallow, but Jack is already moving. His fist slams sweetly into the point of Hammond's jaw with all the force of Jack's more than human speed. With anyone else, it would have knocked them out, maybe even killed them. With Hammond, it just knocks him down.

"Quick," Jack yells. "We need to stop him."

I find myself thinking of the apocalypse. Of how we tried to stop him, and then, with the shadow of his true self around him, we weren't able to do it. Bullets didn't stop him then. How can we stop him now?

"We need to stop him before he can take his true form, all of you," Jack says, aiming a kick at Hammond that keeps him from getting up. "Trust me!"

And that's enough. Because I do trust Jack. I trust him with my life. With all our lives. With the lives of every human being on the planet. I am not going to stand by and let Hammond destroy us. I am not going to believe that I can't stop him, because that is the biggest lie of all those he has ever told.

"Come on," I say to the others, and charge forward.

NINETEEN

I lunge forward, aiming a punch at Hammond. He sways out of the way, but that just sets him up for Grayson to slam into him from the side. Hammond turns, throwing Grayson off, straight at the Fading machine. Grayson hits it with a thud, breaking off part of one of its panels. That doesn't matter now. We're back.

John doesn't join the fight straight away. Instead, he hangs back as Hammond throws a flurry of punches at Jack, almost too quickly to follow, then catches me with a backhanded slap as I try to move in from the side. I stagger, my ears ringing, and I taste blood.

"John, this isn't your father!" I shout. "Come on. You know you were born *here*. And you know what this is!"

Hammond starts to try to change, his skin shifting around him, a glow of power coming up through him. I slam into him, distracting him long enough that he seems to snap back into human form like elastic. If he transforms completely, everyone in our time is dead. He grabs me, his grip crushingly strong.

Finally, John joins the fight, knocking away Hammond's grip. I kick him back and both Jack and Grayson follow it up, backing him into a corner to pummel him with hard strikes. Hammond covers up, protecting himself and blasting through the space between them. I can see him starting to change forms again, so I grab the nearest object, the part Grayson knocked off the Fading machine, and throw it at his head. He bellows furiously as it connects.

"Grab him," Jack yells. "He isn't strong enough to stop all of us."

I nod and rush in. Grayson tackles him low like a football player. It seems that those years on the high school team have finally paid off. Jack hits Hammond higher. I manage to grab an arm, while John latches onto a leg. If we can just keep him pinned down, then we can stop him transforming. We can exhaust him. Wear him down. Even he must get tired.

Suddenly, I'm flying through the air as Hammond throws us off in a burst of strength. I hit something, a wall I think, and slide down, while Hammond gets to his feet. I know that if we don't stop him, he'll transform, but right now, it's hard to even get back to my feet.

Figures burst into the room, dressed in dark body armor and carrying stun guns. I recognize the woman at their head as Rosie Fowler, Jack's second in command when it comes to security. Her pretty features are set in a look of concentration, while her dark hair is cut short and her deep brown eyes are locked onto the scene, trying to take it in. She looks so much older now. No, I realize, she looks the same age she did before. It's me who's younger, leaving her older than all of us. Even Jack.

Rosie gestures, and a couple of the soldiers grab me, pulling me from the room despite my protests. Jack, Grayson and John follow.

"I'm glad to see you're back," Rosie says. "Madam President... um, you look very different."

"It's a long story," I say, managing to focus for a moment or two. "One there isn't enough time for."

"We have to deal with the situation in there, Rosie," Jack explains.

"We've got it, Jack," Rosie insists. She doesn't understand yet. "I mean, we've handled things the last couple of years okay. We knew that we had to hold on while you went back to deal with the Fever. What happened back there, anyway?"

"That's another long story," Grayson supplies.

Jack shakes his head. "Rosie, you don't understand the seriousness of this situation."

Behind us, in the room with the Fading machine, I can hear the sounds of violence. Thuds, the buzz of stun guns, the crack of real ones. Screams.

"The team members don't know how to deal with him," Jack continues. "He isn't human. They don't know what they're getting into."

"What *are* they getting into that it has you so worried?" Rosie asked. "My guys... *our* guys are the best of the best. What more do they need?"

"They need to keep him from transforming," I say. "He... he's the Devil, Rosie."

194

Rosie starts to laugh, and then stops, staring at me with something like horror. "The Devil. You... you're serious, aren't you? What *happened* back there?"

"There still isn't any time," I say, "but Wilson Hammond caused the apocalypse. He stood in the middle of a room, transformed into something... something that gives me nightmares just thinking about it, and called down a rain of fire. We *cannot* let him do the same here. Do you..."

I'm cut off by the sound of an explosion from within the room. Not just the sound, though. I can feel the force of it rippling over us as the doors blow off their hinges, even part of the frame coming away from the wall.

"We have to get you to safety, Ma'am," Rosie says, reaching out for me. I step aside.

"No," I say. "We have to deal with this, or *nowhere* will be safe again."

Jack and Grayson lead the way back into the lab room, but I'm not far behind them. The members of Rosie's team lie scattered around like rag dolls, some injured, others not moving at all. Hammond crouches in the middle of it all. There's blood on his shirt and he's breathing heavily. I don't know what happened in here. Did Hammond do this? Did one of the soldiers, realizing how desperate the situation was, use a grenade?

Hammond rises unsteadily to his feet. He's bleeding from a dozen wounds, none of which seem to have stopped him, but the cumulative effect of which is to slow him down at least. This is our chance. Our chance to finally stop him. It's a chance we didn't take back in the past, because I couldn't see what Hammond was then until it was too late. Now, in our time, it seems like I'm getting a second opportunity to make things right. To save what's left of humanity.

Hammond is back on his feet now. He tears away his shirt, and it's an almost animal gesture, showing the wounds that zigzag across his torso, but which are already starting to close. No, they aren't closing. The rippling of Hammond's flesh isn't that. He's transforming. Already, I can see the beginnings of horns taking shape on his forehead, the nubs of leathery wings rising from his back.

We have to stop him. There were so few survivors the first time he brought down fire and brimstone. In a world ravaged by the Fever, where even our largest population centers are still smaller than the ones they had in the past, there will be no surviving this time. Hammond, or the creature inside him, will finally get his wish. Humanity will be gone.

No. I won't allow that. I can't allow that. Whatever it takes. Even if it kills me. And I have the tool to stop him. A tool I've been so afraid of before. A tool I thought was evil, yet what I'm planning to do with it now is anything but that. I've spent months now controlling my emotions, trying not to get too upset for fear of what will rise in response, but now I dive down into everything I feel, feeding the flames within me.

There's anger. Anger at all the people who have died. Dr. Cook. Dr. Florence. Jonah and so many, many Faders. Lionel, who didn't deserve to die despite how terrified he was of me. All the billions of innocent men, women and children who died in the first apocalypse. Every death is a burst of fuel I use to stoke the fires that sit inside me. But it's more than anger. It's love too. It's the fact that I care about the people who will die if I don't do this. It's the fact that Jack and Grayson are standing in this room, counting on me...

197

Fever (FADE #4)

I glow. I glow with power.

"You think that will stop me?" Hammond demands. "I have the flames of Hell at my command."

"In your human form? You have modern flame retardant materials," I counter. "Or you *had*."

I can see the sudden look of terror on Hammond's face as I reach out for him, throwing myself at him in an embrace. He created the Others to watch out for people like me, maybe not even knowing why he was doing it. He tried to destroy us, calling us a danger to the world. I'm willing to bet that there's a reason he did that. That if he was scared enough to try to kill me, it wasn't without a cause.

I hold to him, clamping onto his clammy, almost leathery flesh. Almost. He hasn't transformed yet. He's still human, trapped in a human body for all his power. I'm burning hotter now than I've burned before, because this close I can feel the hatred. Feel the jealousy that makes him want to destroy us. I scream as I think of the pain and suffering he has inflicted on people. I scream as I *see* it, because this close, it's like I can see into Hammond's mind.

Maybe he wants me to see. Maybe he thinks that seeing what's in there will drive me mad.

It doesn't drive me mad. It *makes* me mad, and I burn all the hotter because of it. Hammond must have been right about being tougher than a human, because it's only now that he starts to scream. It's only now that his flesh burns white hot as I cling to him, not caring if this heat is going to be enough to burn me too. This is what I'm for. This moment, clinging to him, everything I am pouring into him at temperatures that would make the heart of the sun seem cool by comparison.

I stare, just for an instant, into Wilson Hammond's eyes. "Be gone. You are not welcome here, Beast."

There isn't enough time to say more than that, because in that moment, Wilson Hammond is gone. What there is of him burns, and I hold to it while it burns, but I don't have to hold to it for long. With this much heat, in a matter of seconds there is nothing but ash. There's as little left of Wilson Hammond as there was of the first people I burned, what seems like a lifetime ago.

There's a difference though. For once, just for once, I don't feel any horror at what I've done. I don't feel like my humanity is slipping away, or like my power is a curse. For once, it feels like I'm doing what I was always meant to do. Maybe I was. Hammond went to such a lot of trouble to find me. Maybe he knew that this was how it might end. Maybe we both knew in the moment I burned him that it was my destiny.

I stand there looking at the ashes remaining after I've burned him, and I smile. I smile, because finally, it's over.

TWENTY

Jack moves to hold me. No one else could right now. Maybe that's a sign too. He puts his arms around me and gently moves me away from the ashes on the ground.

"It's over, Celes. You can stop burning now. It's all over."

Until he says that, I don't realize that I have tears in my eyes, falling down onto my cheeks and then bubbling up as instant steam. It's over.

"It's over?"

Even saying it like that, it's hard to believe. I cling onto Jack. We've been through the apocalypse together. We've stopped another one. All in less than a week. Or a few thousand years, depending on how you're inclined to count the time. For *us* it was a week, and that's kind of all that matters. Us.

The burning goes back into me so easily this time. Normally, I have to fight to put it back in whatever box that talent lives in within me. Now though, it goes as easily as a sword being put back in a scabbard. It's done what it was needed for. It's done the most important thing it will ever be needed for, I hope.

Suddenly, I'm tired. So very tired. Part of it is the sheer energy I've just put into destroying Hammond. That makes me sag against Jack so that he has to support me just to stop me from collapsing to the floor. There's more to it than that though. So much more. We've been running around almost constantly for months now. In the last few months of my time, I've had to run from secret organizations, infiltrate bases, fight battles I didn't know anything about, and come to terms with an ability that seemed utterly horrifying most of the times I used it.

Now, suddenly, it's over. All that rushing, done, just like that. It's like all the effort of it is catching up to me at once, now that I'm finally, *finally* able to stop. It's exhausting, but it feels good somehow too. Hopeful. Everything I've done has been to try to make things better for my people, and we've succeeded. We've actually done what we set out to do.

I look round at the others. At Jack, Grayson, Johnny. Even at Rosie, stuck back here while the rest of us went off into the past. I love these people. My team. The people who have done so much, and risked so much, to save this world. Even the soldiers currently scattered around the room. *Especially* them, because some of them have given up their lives for this, staying loyal even when it must have looked like we weren't coming back. Sometimes it isn't just about the people doing the exciting part of things. Sometimes it's about the people holding things together back home too.

That thought snaps me out of my exhaustion a little. "I'm fine," I say. "Rosie, get help and get your team to the infirmary."

"Yes, ma'am," Rosie says, snapping off a salute. She and a couple of her team who are strong enough to walk start to help the others out of there. They pause at a couple and shake their heads. I try not to think about what saving our world has cost them, even though I can't help thinking that it has been worth it.

"Grayson," I say, looking at him now. "I'm fine to stand on my own now. I need you to go start rounding people up for a meeting. I'm pretty sure that by this point, everyone will be wondering what is going on here, and seeing you will help to hurry things along. You're in the best position to organize all this. We can give them the news of how the mission went and get up to speed on what's been happening here."

Grayson nods. "Whatever you need, Celes."

He turns and heads for the door. It occurs to me as he goes that things are probably going to be complicated again in the near future. There are going to be meetings, decisions to make, and probably arguments. I might even have to spend time proving that I am who I say I am. After all, I don't exactly look the same right now.

In other words, everything is going to be back to its normal high speed whirl. The world doesn't stop, even when you've just saved it. Yet for now, for a little while at least, I can enjoy the moment. I want to find out exactly how well we've succeeded, though.

"John," I say. "We've changed things, but I need to know how *much* we've changed things. You're in the best position to understand the data. Go check on the Fever. If we're lucky, we'll have destroyed it completely, but I'm worried about that. Rosie seemed to know about it, and if we'd gotten rid of it completely, then she wouldn't. I just hope that we did enough to weaken it. Maybe we can finally deal with it."

John nods. "I hope so. We'll see results, I'm sure of it. If we've reduced the numbers of those creatures, we'll have reduced the disease stock the Fever could evolve from. And with Hammond gone…"

I hadn't thought of that. The Fever was one of Hammond's weapons. One he no doubt had a huge role in maintaining. With him gone, will the Fever fade and die like its creator? I hope so.

John runs off, leaving Jack and me as the only two people in the room. It's probably a breach of protection protocols for the president, but I guess that the security teams aren't used to having me around right now. Besides, it means that Jack can turn me to face him, pull me tightly against him, and kiss me with more passion than I'd have believed possible until he does it.

"I'm so glad I'm here with you," Jack says, brushing a strand of my hair aside with a delicate touch of his fingers. "Even when I got into the Fading machine, I was so scared. I thought... I thought we might be separated like last time."

I can imagine how terrifying that must have been. Last time, we landed years apart. And what if he'd forgotten me, or I'd forgotten him? I know I have to check.

"Jack, can you remember everything?"

"Everything," Jack assures me, with a gentler kiss that nevertheless sends sparks running along my nerve endings. "Every moment with you. Every inch of you."

"That isn't everything," I say with a playful laugh.

"I'm pretty sure I remember everything else too," Jack assures me. "I'm just not sure that it matters much right now. So long as I remember the things that count. And so long as I'm here with you. Remembering you but not being near you would be the hardest thing of all."

I kiss him back then, and it feels like we could spend the whole day just doing that. Maybe more. "I would have found a way back to you, Jack, even if it meant putting the Fading machine back together bit by bit to follow you to a new time period."

"That could be fun," Jack suggests. "Pick a time period, Celes, and we could go."

"Here with you is just fine," I say. "Besides, when we're done here, I think we're going to take the Fading machine apart. We've used it for good, but there would be plenty of people who wouldn't."

Jack smiles, cupping my face in his hands. "That's the Celes I know and love. So determined. So strong, but still thinking about everyone else except yourself."

"I think about myself sometimes," I argue.

Jack arches an eyebrow. "Like when?"

"It was pretty selfish of me to jump back after you." I step back from him slightly. "I should have been here running things, but I couldn't stop myself."

"And you saved the world because of it," Jack points out. "Besides, it's kind of nice to know that the woman I love will abandon running the free world to follow me into the past."

"Now though, I have to go back to doing that," I say. It's not such a hardship. Not really. Even so, it does feel a little like a weight pressing down on me as the return to responsibility hits home. "I'll have to go out and reassure the people about the Fever once we have the confirmation from John that we can stop it. Then there will be the meeting with the Cabinet. Do you even think they'll let me go on being president? I mean, physically, I'm a lot younger than I was when I got the job…"

"You're still you," Jack assures me. "Wonderfully, perfectly you. Don't forget that. Don't forget that you've already done a lot of good in this job either."

"Thanks," I say with a smile. "Though I guess I kind of liked being a student, you know?"

"I know," Jack says. "I loved you as president, but I also loved falling back in love with you when I was a Fader, too. I loved the simplicity of that."

I nod. "It looks like the world is going to get complicated again though."

"As complicated as we let it be," Jack insists. "Listen. Everything is going to be fine."

"Even with the Fever?" I can't help a sudden stab of worry at the thought of the Fever. We don't have the results back from John yet. There are still so many things that could have gone wrong. What if the Faders' tactics didn't scare enough of the creatures to death? What if those that did survive were able to breed and grow stronger? What if Hammond did something before he left? Things should be better by now, but what if they aren't?

"It's okay," Jack assures me, taking my hands. "Before he... before he died, Dr. Cook issued orders for the remaining Faders to keep up the fight. He effectively changed their main mission. They went from looking for people like us to looking for the creatures and destroying them wherever they found them. I don't know how well they did, but if they were half as determined about that as they were about hunting us, I'm pretty sure there won't have been many of the creatures surviving."

"I hope so," I say.

Jack smiles. "Sometimes, hope is all we have. Hope and trust. We have to trust the Faders left in the past. We have to trust that the sacrifice of all those people wasn't in vain. We have to trust that the man who was my father for so many years didn't die for nothing."

"I'm so sorry about him," I say, reaching out to hold Jack.

"It's okay," he says. "If we find a way to get past the Fever, it's okay. We get past things. We keep going.

That's what people do, Celes. As long as they keep doing that, there's always hope for the future."

"And us?" I ask.

"I'd like to think that there's plenty of hope for us too."

CHAPTER 21

It takes a while before we can be certain that our trip into the past has done anything. It shouldn't work like that. What we did happened thousands of years ago, after all, but it does. It takes us a couple of weeks at least for John to be able to confirm that there's a weakness in the Fever that we can exploit. A chance of a real cure that grows more real by the day. Pretty soon, we're shipping out medicine, and then vaccines to stop any related strains before they can start.

I say we. Mostly, I'm not doing a lot of the science. I'm just involved in the decision making behind it, running meetings and trying to get our government to work the way we've always had it working. Apparently, disappearing for months on end did a lot of damage, no matter how hard Rosie and the rest of those left behind worked to keep things going.

Fever (FADE #4)

I have to spend a lot of that time assuring people that I *am* Celestra Caine, the woman they voted for. That seems to happen more in meetings with other politicians than elsewhere. With them, I'm meeting with mostly older men and women, so it takes me a while to convince them that I'm not a joke. My meeting with the French ambassador was a long one. Generally though, eventually, they get the message. I'm me, the country is running as it was, and if they have any sense, they shouldn't try to take advantage of the fact that I don't look very old. Especially not with Jack standing behind me.

The people are a lot more forgiving. More than that, they seem to *like* the idea of a president who looks this young, while still having the experience for the job. Or maybe they just like the idea of a commander in chief willing to risk her own life to deal with a threat that was going to kill them all.

It's still at least a couple more weeks before I'm in a position to order the military to sweep for the hybrid creatures behind the Fever, though. A sweep like that, over the entire country, takes time to set up, especially when doing it in between assuring politicians that I'm still alive and in charge.

When we finally do it, the results are everything I could have hoped for. There's no sign of the creatures, meaning that whatever strain of the Fever we have is just a weaker disease that drifted in to fill the gap left by the change in history. No wonder John and his people are having such a good time of curing people now, compared with before.

I sit in my office contemplating that fact. Jack's there too, by my side, the way he always is.

"It looks like the Faders got the creatures," I say.

Jack nods, and then smiles broadly. It's probably the warmest grin I've seen from him. "I knew they would. I knew *we* would. How does it feel to have averted the biggest disaster in the history of this country?"

I don't know. At least, I don't have the words for it. Thankfully, Jack doesn't seem very interested in words right now. He kisses me lightly on the tip of the nose.

"We should relax. Find a way to celebrate."

Fever (FADE #4)

I can guess what he has in mind, but before we can go anywhere with it, Grayson is in the room. He walks over.

"Madam President, we have a situation that requires your attention in the grand ballroom."

"What kind of a situation?" I ask. What could it be? Something new from the past? Some problem with the Fever? We've only just gotten things back to normal.

"It's better if you come see it," Grayson says. "You too, Jack."

He leads the way across to double doors flanked by guards, which open to reveal a ballroom set out for dining, with long tables and a vast spread of food. There are people standing by the tables, looking over at us. Obviously waiting for us.

"Surprise!" That's loud enough that I cry out in shock at it. I wasn't expecting anything like *this*.

Grayson pushes us gently inside. The members of the Cabinet are all there. So are Rosie and John, dignitaries from several different countries, important people from around the United States and more. Some of them look like just regular citizens. That's good. I always hate the

214

idea of being shut away from ordinary people like we're somehow meant to be better than them.

"We've been planning this almost since we got back," Grayson says. "It's the kind of event that needs celebrating properly. After all, it isn't every day that you get to save the world."

"You did all this?" I ask.

"Me and a few others. It wasn't easy keeping it from you and Jack, you know how sharp he is around secrets, but I figured, with how busy you'd both been, you deserved it."

A pretty brunette in her thirties comes up to me. It's Liza, one of the aides who works in the building. "Madam President, I didn't get a chance to say it when you first came back, but we're all so grateful for what you did, and so happy that you came back okay."

"I'm glad to be back," I assure her.

She gestures to where the guests have lined up. "If you'd like to get the introductions out of the way now, we can get on with the party afterwards?"

"That would be good," I say. Liza introduces me to a lot of the visiting dignitaries, most of whom I have met before now, often while pleading for help with the Fever. Most of them are a lot more friendly than they were then. Maybe they've worked out that, now that we aren't going to be spending all our time fighting this disease, we'll be able to concentrate on rebuilding.

"Now for the civilians," Liza says with a smile. "They've been hand selected, and most of them are very excited about meeting you."

"Which is Liza's way of saying that it's show time," Jack says softly. "I'll see you in a little while, Celes. There are a couple of things I need to take care of."

Liza starts me towards the ordinary people, introducing me to the first couple, but Grayson quickly takes over, leaving the aide free to go eat and mingle. He gets me through the line of people I'm meant to be meeting, then as the part actually turns *into* a party, he leads me outside onto one of the balconies with a view out over the White House grounds.

He reaches out to touch my face. It's something I can remember him doing back when we were running track together, but he hasn't done it since we got back. I

216

miss that life. I miss that Grayson. I miss a lot of things, including being with him.

"Celes," Grayson reaches down to take my hands. "We've been so busy recently that I've hardly seen anything of you, but the truth is that I haven't known what to say to you. I know it's not the best time, but I have to say what's in my heart. I have to say it, so that we'll both know where we stand."

"Grayson..."

"No," he says, "please don't interrupt. I need to say this. You know we were lovers before all this. And you know I've always loved you. You know from when we were back there how good things could be. I'd always wondered that, but I've also found myself wondering what things would have been like for us if Jack had still been around. Would it have happened? I know you care about me, but I need to know how much you care about me."

"What are you saying?" I ask him, even though I think I can guess.

Grayson looks a little nervous then. He runs his fingers through his hair, smoothing it out. "I loved every moment that I got to spend with you, Celes, but if there

217

are going to be any more, I need to know that it's real. I don't want to be your second best. I don't want to be the guy you go to just because Jack isn't there."

He takes my hands, kissing my fingers one by one. "I need to know how things stand now that we're all back here. Now that you have a real choice. You've been in relationships with both of us, and both Jack and I are dangling on the hook right now, not knowing what's going to happen next. Who do you love, Celes?"

"I love both of you," I say.

Grayson sighs. "I know. But you know what I'm asking. Which of us do you want to spend your life with? Do you love me the way I love you? Do you want me more than anything? Will I ever be first for you?"

Grayson looks so vulnerable in that moment that I want to reach out to wipe away the worry from his face. I want to tell him that everything is going to be okay. Because I do love him. This wouldn't be such a big deal if I didn't love him at least a little. But loving him the way he loves me? More than that, do I love him the way I love Jack?

218

The answer to that is so simple. No. I don't. I love Grayson with the kind of warm love that grows from spending so much time around someone that it's impossible to feel any other way. I want him as my friend for the rest of my life, but he isn't... he isn't Jack Simple.

Jack makes my heart beat faster just thinking about him. I loved him before I went back into the past. I loved him in the past, not even knowing who he really was. I love him now. I love him with a fire to match the one inside me. I love him, and I know I'll love him until the day I die. I couldn't be me and not love Jack like that.

Grayson doesn't even need me to say anything. I can see the emotions flickering across his features. Surprise, anger, and finally a kind of resigned sadness.

"Grayson," I say, "you're one of the most important people in my life. I don't want to lose what you bring to my life, but..."

"But I'm not him," Grayson says.

I shake my head. "No, you're not him, and it's him I love."

"Faded or not, it seems like there's no way I can win," Grayson says. "I guess, if it had to be anyone, I'm

219

glad it's Jack. If there's anyone else worthy of you, it's him. I'll still be around, I guess, and I wish you and Jack the best. If anyone deserves to be happy, it's the two of you, but for now…"

He kisses me softly, one last time. He's kissing me goodbye and I know it. I don't know if our friendship will survive this moment. I hope so.

The tears come then. I can't stop them. I never planned this, even though I've known for so long that it has been coming, one way or the other. I've tried to balance the two of them, but that has just made things worse. It's let Grayson come deeper and deeper into his relationship with me, until I've finally had to tell him that there is no relationship. I hate myself right now.

"It's okay," Grayson says, and I hug him, holding him close. Wanting to say that everything is the way he wants it to be, but knowing that I can't.

Eventually, I have to pull back. We both do, even though it might be the last time we hold one another like that. I look up… and that's when I see Jack standing there, watching us.

"Jack!"

220

It's too late. He turns and stalks from the room without a word.

EPILOGUE

Two days. Two days, and I somehow can't manage to sit down and talk with Jack. I'm the President of the United States of America. I can arrange sit down meetings with almost any leader on the planet. I *have* meetings arranged with half of them, mostly about the way my country is going to be going in the wake of the Fever crisis. All that, yet somehow, I can't manage to talk to the one person I really need to.

A lot of that is up to Jack. I couldn't catch him when he left the party. He slipped through the room too fast, leaving me to be slowed down by people demanding "just a minute" of my time. Since then, he has been... gone. He hasn't disappeared, exactly, but he never seems to be there. Whenever I've gone looking for him, he's been out on a trip to assess the damage or the rebuilding efforts.

For a man whose job is meant to be at my side, he's suddenly gone from it a lot.

Is it over between us? I saw the way he reacted. I saw his face in that moment. Does he think that I chose Grayson over him? Does he not want anything more to do with me? That thought physically hurts. The idea that I could have pushed Grayson aside because I love Jack so much, only for Jack to decide that he doesn't love me is too much. It's too much even for me to concentrate on my work properly. Several times now, I've read reports or had meetings, only to realize afterwards that I haven't taken any of it in.

I don't know what my advisors and aides must think. They probably think that I really am the teenage girl I appear to be, and that I shouldn't be dealing with the running of the country if I can't even deal with something like this. Yet the truth is, no matter how old I appeared to be when it happened, Jack refusing to talk to me would stop me in my tracks.

"Madam President?" Liza has come into the Oval Office, waiting in front of my desk while I snap out of my thoughts. I'm staring down at a report on economic output that I should be taking very seriously indeed, but haven't been able to concentrate on.

"What is it, Liza?" That comes out harsher than I intended. Anyone who has intruded on me and my thoughts of Jack in the last couple of days has gotten the same, but I realize now how bad it must make me look. These people don't deserve it. They've kept the country running while I've been away in the past. They shouldn't have to deal with this as well.

"I'm sorry, Liza," I say with a sigh. "I know I can't have been much fun to work with, the past couple of days. What do you need?"

"Your presence is required in the rose gardens," Liza says, with a slight smile. Is that because of the apology?

"In the rose gardens? I don't remember an appointment for now. Certainly not one there. What's going on?"

Liza shakes her head. "I think I'm going to have to risk my job by refusing to answer that one, Madam President."

I look at her a little longer, trying to make some kind of sense of it. Liza reaches out to touch my shoulder.

"Just go," she says. "Trust me."

I stand up, deciding that whatever the situation is, it can't be any harder to deal with than the ones I've already dealt with. After all, between us, Jack, Johnny, Grayson and I have stopped the Fever, prevented another apocalypse, and dealt with Wilson Hammond. Next to that, almost anything is simple. Though it generally involves a lot more meetings.

Liza leads the way down to the rose gardens, a couple of secret service agents flanking us on the way down. Even that has me thinking about Jack and the way he would stay with me, protecting me through everything. The times when I've been most lost have been the times when he hasn't been near me. I don't think I can bear this now. What if he never agrees to speak to me? What if he doesn't believe me when I tell him that I was breaking things off with Grayson? After all the times Grayson and I *have* kissed, would I believe it if I were Jack?

I shake my head, trying to focus on the meeting ahead of me. It must be pretty important to get an unscheduled slot with me. Liza is pretty ferocious when it comes to protecting time in my calendar. Apparently, merely being in possession of a functioning time machine doesn't change anything when it comes to the amount of time I have available. I realize I'm thinking about nonsense to keep from thinking about anything else.

Liza takes me as far as the gate to the rose gardens. Even the secret service agents stay behind there. That's unusual. I step in, thinking for a moment about how beautiful the evening is, and how good the garden looks right now. In fact, it looks better than good. There are fairy lights set up around the garden, shining like miniature stars among the roses and making them seem to glow translucently in the fading light. It's such a beautiful, calm space. When did I last get the time to come down here?

I walk through the gardens, up towards a gazebo set to look out over the small lake in the grounds. It's all so serene and still. More peaceful than I feel right now. I sit down in the gazebo, looking out and trying to let some of that peace flow through me. I should feel peaceful. It's over. It's done. Yet that isn't how the world works. Not really.

226

I hear the light tread of footsteps nearby and look up. Jack's there. He's wearing a grey suit that is cut perfectly to emphasize his toned, muscular frame. He stands so elegantly. So perfectly poised. He looks almost exactly the way he looked the first time I saw him in his apartment, dressed as a Fader.

He's breathtaking. Maybe it's just not seeing him for a couple of days, or maybe it's how much I want things to be right between us, but he looks perfect standing there, his features chiseled, those pale, pale eyes, on me. As always with Jack, I can't even begin to guess at what he's feeling.

At least until he moves closer, tilting my head up so that he can kiss me.

It's a kiss like coming home. A kiss that I've been imagining for almost two days straight now. Jack's mouth is on mine and it's all I can do to hold myself back from pulling him down beside me in the gazebo. Jack seems to sense that too, because he puts his hands gently on my shoulders, pulling me to my feet before stepping back.

"Celes," he says, "I've been doing a lot of thinking. I've been thinking about my father, and all the regrets he

227

had when my mother passed away. I've been thinking about everything we've done. I've been thinking about you, too."

"Jack…"

"I don't want any regrets," Jack says. "We've dealt with Hammond and the rest of it, but we have no way of knowing what might be coming tomorrow. If I walk away from you now, I'll regret that for the rest of my life. We might not get a chance to make it right."

"I love you, Jack," I say.

"And I love you. I've never known a time when I *haven't* loved you. We found each other even when we didn't know who we were. We fell in love again without knowing it. That's what matters."

"I was saying goodbye to Grayson, Jack," I say. "I was telling him that I love you too much to ever be with him."

"I know," Jack says. "He told me. That's why I've spent most of the last couple of days trying to make this perfect."

"You've been doing *what*?" I ask. "I thought you were angry with me. I thought you hated me."

228

"I could never hate you," Jack promises me. He smiles. "And as for making me angry... well, you've managed to do that plenty of times when you've put yourself at risk. I haven't run away from you then, have I?"

"Then what..." I begin. I think about what he has just said. "What were you making perfect?"

Jack takes my hand. "We've done a lot of things," he says. "And we've bent a lot of rules doing them. I think that one more won't hurt. I might be your head of security, but I also love you too much to just be an occasional thing for you. We belong together, and I want to be with you completely. Forever."

"What are you saying?" I ask Jack breathlessly. I think I know, but I need to hear it from him.

Jack falls to one knee, taking a box out of his pocket. He opens it to reveal a ring that shines with a fire that matches the one within us.

"This is where you've been the last couple of days?" I ask.

Jack nods. "Will you marry me, Celes? Will you make me the happiest man in this or any other time?"

Fever (FADE #4)

I freeze there as he actually says it. I know what I want, and what I want to say, but right now, getting the words out is hard. It's hard to say how much I love him. How much I need him. Because words just don't seem to do it justice right now. Nothing seems to. I stare at Jack's features. So strong, so handsome. So sure, even in the face of the greatest dangers. The kind of man who could be beside me through anything.

It's about more than that too, I realize, as a little of the confidence slips out of Jack's expression. There are lots of action men out there, but Jack is the one whose sensitive side is there too. He loves me, purely and absolutely. He'd do anything for me. I think back to the times we shared in the apartment together, pretending to be boyfriend and girlfriend. To all the times we've spent when bullets haven't been flying towards us. Those have been the times when I've seen the real Jack Simple.

And I love him.

"Celes?" Jack says, still down on one knee.

I reach down, pulling him up and kissing him softly. Gently. I whisper it into his ear, just between the two of us.

"Yes. Yes, Jack, I'll marry you."

Jack pulls back just enough to slide the ring onto my finger. It's perfect, a little like Jack. It seems so hard and cold on the outside, yet in just the right light, I can see the fire inside it. It's beautiful. Though not quite as beautiful as he is. I don't think anyone is.

Jack takes me in his arms then. "If we're going to be together," he says, "then I don't think we should waste any more time, do you?"

I smile at him. "What exactly do you have in mind, Jack Simple?"

He answers me with a deep kiss that seems to set my body on fire. That's good, because it's pretty much what I had in mind too. To start with, anyway.

*****

This concludes the FADE Series. Thank you for taking this ride through FADE with me and with many other readers. I hope you'd enjoyed FADE as much as I enjoyed writing it.

If you'd enjoyed this series, let me, my publishers, and other readers know by writing a review. Who knows, there may be another book in the future...

For updates on whether there is a spin-off or more books in the future for FADE, visit Sparklesoup.com and sign up for new releases.

Kailin Gow

Falling (FADE #2)

Forgotten (FADE #3)

Fever (FADE #4)

Available at all bookstores!

Kailin Gow

A FINAL WORD

Reasons Why?

I get asked this all the time, why do you interact with your readers so much?

1) The answer is simply because I see many of my readers as friends.

I'm a reader, too, and over the years, I've gotten to know some of you through Facebook, Twitter, or even at events I'm participating in. You have read my books, understood the story, and have come to love the characters in these stories as much as I do.

Over the years, I've gotten to know many of my readers. I share your pain when you lose a love one, congratulate you on victories, go through your birthdays and dramas at home and work. So you see, in other words, a lot of my readers have become friends of mine. You read my books, and even understand me like a friend understands a friend.

2) I know how reading can be time-consuming so I am pretty happy when a reader Facebook me and tells me she just read one of my books and she knows she'll be one of my biggest fans. I can't tell you how incredibly touched I

235

am when someone tells me this. It literally brings tears to my eyes.

Not only does this feel incredible, and I am truly honored, but I want my readers to know from the bottom of my heart, this:

3) You Make Me, an Author, feel Warm and Fuzzy, too!

When you love my books and even reach out to me to let me know how much you love my books or that it has touched you in some way, and even write a review about it, you can't imagine how happy that makes me. I'm only human you know. It makes me feel good about what I'm working hard for.

4) My Readers are Not Only Interesting, but they are Fun, Smart, and Great to Hang Out with!

So, please don't be a stranger. Come on by and say "Hi" on Twitter, Facebook, or my blogs. And become a Facebook friend of mine and vice versa. I really do want to find out more about you, and consider it a great honor that you're a reader of mine.

From the bottom of my humble heart:

Kailin Gow

THANK YOU!

You can find me at:

Website: http://www.kailingow.com

Facebook:
http://www.facebook.com/OfficialKailinGow

Instagram:
http://instagram/kailingow

237

From USA Today Bestselling Author for
Young Adults

Kailin Gow

comes

PULSE

Kailin Gow

17 year-old Kalina didn't know her boyfriend was a vampire until the night he died of a freak accident. She didn't know he came from a long line of vampires until the night she was visited by his half-brothers Jaegar and Stuart Graystone. There were a lot of secrets her boyfriend didn't tell her. Now she must discover them in order to keep alive. But having two half-brothers vampires around had just gotten interesting...

EXCERPT FROM

PULSE

By Kailin Gow

****

prologue

She ran like an animal. Her clothes were wet, sopping, clinging to her thighs and to her chest, hollow and transparent around the curve of her shoulders. Her hair shook out droplets of rain; her cheeks were flushed and she was breathless. He could see her heartbeat throbbing at the side of her throat, see it in the rhythmic panting, hear it from across the street, pounding in his ears, intermingled with the thunder bolting from the sky. He could feel it – it felt like an earthquake to him, shaking his ribs, his shoulders, his legs. It had been so long since he had seen a heartbeat like hers – since he had felt a heartbeat at all.

The skies had opened up – as they so often did in North California – without any warning, without any hesitation. It was as if the smooth blue glass ceiling of the world had shattered all at once, letting the primordial oceans pound down upon the pavement. He could see her consternation, her irritation – she wanted nothing but to get out of the rain, to dry herself off, to curl up into
something warm and dry.

But Jaegar loved the rain. He loved the energy – the pulse of life beating down upon the earth. He could hear the scattered raindrops in their rhythmic approach to earth and pretend that each fall of rain was a beat of his dead heart. And she was alive with the energy, too – *alive* as he had never seen a woman alive, tossing her hair back, running into shelter, and her lips were pink and her cheeks were red. He remembered that his lips would never again be pink, that his cheeks would never again be red.

She was so young.

Humans so often surprised him in that way. They looked no different from him – he could have been seventeen; he had been seventeen for so long – but their youth never failed to surprise him. The way the world was so new to them – that rain could still take them by surprise, when he had seen so many rainfalls.

He could smell her. The wind carried her scent to him like an animal's scent, and it was all he could do to keep his fangs in check. He leaned heavily upon the branch and parted the leaves to get a better look at her. He could feel the blood – stagnant in his veins – begin something like a torpid, sluggish, shift towards life – the closest thing he would ever get to a heartbeat. She was the sort of girl who made young boys' hearts pound, he thought – and they never knew how lucky they were to experience that sensation.

For it was the physical aspect of it, he thought, that humans understood least of all. They romanticized vampires, of course – how terrible it would be to live at night! To drink blood! To prey upon humans! These were things they could intellectualize, understand. Humans had been forced to commit murder. Humans had been forced to bite back their most natural, primal desires – and so they could almost understand, when they imagined vampires, what it was like to feel that insatiable hunger for a woman's throat, her breast, her wrist. But not a human in the world had ever been alive without *living*, without a heartbeat – and so they took it for granted – what it meant, that constant linear throbbing, clock-like, towards inevitable death. For Jaegar was a vampire, and he was not alive, and the dull ache in his chest where a heartbeat should have been was for him one of the most agonizing things in the world.

They don't know, he thought. *They'll never understand.*

He had been told that she was the one. He had waited for her until sunset – the sun agonizing upon him, even with the ring around his finger. Vampires were not meant for light, and even the strongest magic could not take away the pain, searing, burning, aching, in his flesh. He was unnatural in sunlight, and only now that dusk was beginning to settle over him could he find relief. He sat perched in the tree, obscured by the leaves, staring at her as she ran down the street.

He leaned in too closely – the birds noticed at last that something was wrong in their midst and took flight; a flurry of wings beat up around him and the branch snapped from the tree and plummeted to the earth below.

It was enough time to make a distraction.

He concentrated, and in half a second he was behind her, so close he could feel the wind blow her hair upon his lips, and then he opened the umbrella above her.

"Miss," he said.

She startled.

"What the..." She rounded on him.

"You looked wet," he said. She did not seem amused.

"I'm warning you," she said. "I know kung fu."

He had learned kung fu once, many centuries ago. He thought it better not to mention it.

"I'm sorry," he said. "I was just trying to help."

She softened.

"Thanks," she said, lamely. "I'm sorry – I didn't mean to snap at you. But you need to learn not to sneak up on people like that. You scared me."

Her eyes remained fixed upon the tree from which he had come. A suspicious glare clouded her gaze. Had she seen – was she wondering? He knew she knew something was wrong. He tried to maintain whatever pleasant normalcy he could. The sequoias were tall, after all. No human could survive a jump from them – he knew she knew this. He knew she thought he was human.

Kailin Gow

BITTER FROST

All her life, Breena had always dreamed about fairies as though she lived amongst them... beautiful fairies living amongst mortals and living in Feyland. In her dreams, he was always there – the breathtakingly handsome but dangerous Winter Prince, Kian, who is her intended. Then she sees Kian, who seems intent on finding her and carrying her off to Feyland. If she is his intended, why does he seem to hate her and want her dead? And

247

Fever (FADE #4)

her best friend Logan has suddenly become protective.
Things are getting strange…

EXCERPT FROM

BITTER FROST

****

Prologue

The dream had come again, like the sun after a storm. It was the same dream that had come many times before, battering down the doors of my mind night after night since I was a child. It was the sort of dreams all girls dream, I suppose – a dream of mysterious worlds and hidden doorways, of leaves that breathe and make music when they are rustled in the wind, and rivers that bubble and froth with secrets. *Dreams*, my mother always told me, *represent part of our unconsciousness – the place where we store the true parts of our soul, away from the rest of the world.* My mother was an artist; she always thought this way. If it was true, then my true soul was a denizen of this strange and fantastical world. I often felt, in waking hours,

249

that I was in exile, somehow – somehow less myself, less *true*, than I had been in my enchanted slumber. The real world was only a dream, only an echo, and in silent moments throughout the day it would hit me: *I am not at home here.*

I would shake the thought off, of course, dismiss it as stupid, try and apply my mother's armchair psychoanalysis to the situation. But then, before bed, the thought would come to me, trickle through the mire of worries (boys, school, whether or not I'd remembered to charge my IPod before getting into bed, whether or not my banner would be torn down yet again from the homeroom message board) – *will I have the dream tonight?* And then, another thought would come to me alongside it. *Will I be going home again.*

And the night before my sixteenth birthday, the dream came again – stronger and more vivid than it had ever come before, as if the gauzy wisp of a curtain between reality and dream-land had at last been torn open, and I looked upon my fantasy with new eyes.

I was a fairy princess. (When waking, I would chide myself for this fantasy – sixteen-year-old girls should want to start a fruitful career in environmental activism, not twirl around in silk dresses). But I was a fairy princess, and I was a child. I dreamed myself into a palace – with spires reaching up into the sun, so that the rays seemed to pour gold down onto the turrets. The floors were marble; vines bursting with flowers were wrapped around all the colonnades. The halls were covered in mirrors – gold-framed glass after gold-framed glass – and in these hundred kaleidoscopic images I could see my reflection refracted a hundred times.

I was a toddler – perhaps four, maybe five years old, decked out in elaborate jewels, swaddled in lavender silk, yards and yards of the fabric – the color of my eyes. I hated the color of my eyes in real life – their pale color seemed to make me alien and strange – but here, they were beautiful. Here, I was beautiful. Here, I was home.

The music grew louder, and I could hear its melody. It was not like human music – no, not even the most beautiful concertos, most elaborate sonatas. This was the music that humans try to make and fail – the language of the stars as they twinkle, the rhythm of the human heart as it beats, the glimmering harmony of all the planets and all the moons and all the secret melodies of nature. It was a music that haunted me always, whenever I woke up.

Beside me there was a boy – a few years older than I was. I knew his name; somehow my heart had whispered it to my brain. *Kian*. All the palace around me was golden – with peach hues and warm, pulsating life – but Kian was pale, pale like snow. His eyes were icy blue, with just a hint of silver flecked around the irises; his hair was so black that ink itself would drown in it. He seemed out of place in the vernal palace that was my home – out of season with the

251

baskets of ripe fruit that hung down from the ceiling, with the sweet, honey-strong smell of the flowers. But he was beautiful, and all the more beautiful for his strangeness.

We were dancing to the music, our bodies echoing the sounds we heard – or perhaps the sounds were echoing us. We were learning the Equinox Dance. It was the dance that we would dance on our wedding day.

It was a custom in this fairy kingdom that royal children would learn this dance – the most complicated and mysterious of all dances – for their wedding days. And so we all practiced, day after day (night after dream-rich night), for the day that we would come of age, and dance the dance truly, our feet moving in smooth unison, echoing the commingling of our souls.

My father was the fairy king of the Summer Kingdom – a place where everything tasted like honey and felt like the morning sun on your forehead. Kian's mother was the Winter Queen of the Winter Kingdom, a place beyond the mountains where cool breezes turned into arctic chill, where a castle made of amethyst stood upon a rocky peak, and evergreens dotted the horizon. And it was only fitting that our two kingdoms should meet, should join together; we were the chosen ones.

"You will be my Queen," the boy whispered to me. His voice was confident, strong.

The dance was still difficult for us. I got tangled in my waves of lavender satin, tripping over his silver shoes.

He in turn kept fumbling with his hands, trying to spin me around the waist and instead, elbowing me in the side – but somehow it didn't hurt.

"Silly," cried the other girl watching us. She, like Kian, was stunning – her hair was as long and lustrous as a starless night; her eyes were silver, like the pelt of a wolf. She was called Shasta, I knew. "Silly – that's not how you dance." She giggled, and her eyes glittered with her laugh.

And then everything changed and became chaos – my home was suddenly ripped apart and replaced by a new scene. Something – *something* – was attacking, something with teeth and horns and claws that ripped, something that made a great and bellowing sound I could hear even when I pressed my hands tightly to my ears. *The Minotaur.*

The screaming came from all directions; everybody was running – me and Shasta and Kian – and the adults, all of them – away from the Minotaur, into each other. Everyone had gone mad. And then someone – someone – was fighting it, a cavalcade of fairy knights each shining in his golden armor – and some knights from the Winter Kingdom too, in their silver.

The Summer King and Queen were there, and the Winter Queen was there too. She looked like Shasta, but older – and her face was different. There was something hard and glinting in her eyes that I could not see in Shasta's, like the shiny specks in stone. I was afraid.

253

Fever (FADE #4)

"This is your fault!" a voice snapped – I could not tell to whom it belonged.

"No – it's yours!" Another voice – equally angry, equally cold.

"If it hadn't been for your kingdom..."

"Don't give me those excuses – the Minotaur is a device of your court!"

The voices grew higher and stranger, angrier, louder, quicker and quicker in their retorts until I felt like I was surrounded in a cacophony of rage, bellowing over and over again until at last all I heard was:

"It's all because of that girl!"

And for a moment, they were all silent, and all of them were staring at me.

I could not understand, but it did not matter. Before I could think, could understand what was going on, what was happening to me, the scene had changed again.

I felt his arms around me. That was the first thing; I felt it before I could see anything, see him. I felt his arms encircle my shoulders, feel him brushing my shoulder blades lightly with his fingertips. I shivered. His hands took mine. I could see him. It was Kian, but he was older, now, and so was I – both a young man and a young woman – staring at each other. Age had only made us more beautiful; his hair was longer, now, and his eyes sharper, with greater depth. I could see my reflection in his eyes; my hair was longer too: a deep, warm brown with flecks of gold studded throughout. And I could see my expression – full of fear, full of joy – as he bent down closer to me, as his lips came ever closer to mine.

"Oh, Breena," he said to me. "My Breena."

His blue eyes took on a look of sharp determination; he stared at me with such intensity that I felt that his eyes had penetrated into the truest part of my true soul, a part hidden even to the rest of this strange and wonderful land.

"I will kill you, Breena. It is what I have to do. It is decreed." He cupped my face with his hands, and I could feel his cool breath whispering upon my cheek. "We are mortal enemies."

Always, every night, that same dream – that same fear, that same joy. When I woke up each morning, I felt a profound sense of loss, a yearning that stretched so deeply it crossed the bounds of reality itself. The alarm clock would ring, and everything would change. I was a nearly-sixteen-year-old girl, with suede boots, with T-shirts bearing sayings I believe in." I had an IPod, a cell phone, my laptop (with pages full of html code for my brainchild, teensforgreatergood.com). I spoke in rushed slang about the latest films and television shows, played video games with Logan, teased him when he won, teased him when he lost. I wore little to no makeup and complained about homework during G-Format. The idea of dating – of fumbling high school boys trying to score in between stolen keg stands, of

Facebook relationship statuses and hastily-texted endearments – repulsed me.

But for a few hours each night, I was somebody else. I was a princess in a castle, with a dress made of lavender and besides me there is a prince with arctic-blue eyes, and arms wrapped closely around me, and lips coming nightly ever closer to mine...

I was home.

Kailin Gow

Other Books By Kailin Gow

Fantasy Romance Series
<u>FROST SERIES</u>
<u>Age 15 and Up</u>

Bitter Frost and The Wolf Fey
Forever Frost
Silver Frost
Frost Kisses
Midnight Frost
Frost Fire
Spring Frost
Enchanted Frost
Ring of Ice
Ring of Fire
The Fairy Letters

The Wolf Fey: Frost Series Spin-Off
Age 15 and Up

The Wolf Fey
The Red Wolf
Wolf Magic

The Fairy Rose Chronicles
(FROST Series that Takes Place 5 Years Earlier than the Bitter Frost Series)
AGE 9 and Up

The Fairy Rose
Fairy Fair (Fairy Rose Chronicles #2)
Pixies vs. Fairies (Fairy Rose Chronicles #3)

DESIRE
Age 17 and Up

Desire
Summer Wishes
Shattered
Passion

FADE
Age 15 and Up

FADE
Falling
Forgotten
Fever

Wicked Woods Series
Age 15 and Up

Wicked Woods
Shimmer
Silver
Silence
Sight
Shifter

Alchemists Academy Series
Age 13 and Up

Stones to Ashes
Elemental Explosions
The Quantum Games
The Year of the Elite

Kailin Gow

Wordwick Games Series (An SAT-Prep Series)
Age 15 and Up

Rise of the Fire Tamer
The Ascension
The Return

Want More Edgy books for Teens and Up like this one?

Enter

Sparklesoup Teens

Sparklesoup.com/Teens

Where you will find edgy books for teens, young adults, and new adults that would make your heart pound, your skin crawl, and leave you wanting more...

Feed Your Reading Addiction

www.ingramcontent.com/pod-product-compliance
Lightning Source LLC
Chambersburg PA
CBHW052044240626

47153CB00006B/2203